A Vicarage Reunion

A Vicarage Reunion

A Holley Sisters of Thornthwaite Novel

KATE HEWITT

TULE
PUBLISHING

Chapter One

"ESTHER!"

Her mother's tone of pleased surprise morphed into confusion, and then, predictably, worry, as her kindly face creased with concern. "Why have you got a suitcase?"

"Two suitcases," Esther Langley answered, and hefted both as she stood on the stone steps, the March wind cold and damp as it buffeted her. "May I come in?"

"Of course, darling. You don't have to knock. You usually don't." Her mother's forehead was furrowed as she stepped aside so Esther could walk into the Victorian tiled porch of her childhood home, the vicarage of Thornthwaite, a village of two thousand hardy souls nestled at the foot of Lonscale Fell in England's Lake District.

Esther put the suitcases down in the porch and her mother glanced at them askance. "Shall I put on the kettle?"

Esther nodded in relief, grateful for the momentary reprieve from her mother's well-meaning concern. "Please."

She followed her mother down the hall and around the back of the Georgian house to the kitchen, the cosy heart of the home. The family's elderly black lab, Charlie, was sprawled in his usual place in front of the rather battered Aga, and there was a smell of sugar and spice in the air.

"I've just made some Bakewell tarts for the pop-in morning in the church hall," Ruth said as she filled the electric kettle and switched it on. "But they can spare two, I think."

"Thanks, Mum." Esther let out a hefty sigh and sank into one of the colourful, mismatched chairs at the table of scarred oak where she'd eaten countless childhood meals. It felt both good and awful to be back in her childhood home at aged thirty-five, enveloped in the sweet-smelling warmth of the kitchen, yet with a leaden weight of sadness and disappointment in her stomach.

Ruth didn't ask any prying questions as she made the tea, and Esther rested her chin in her hands, feeling absolutely shattered but knowing she couldn't show up at the vicarage with two suitcases and no explanations. Her mother deserved to know why she was here. In any case, her life's trials would inevitably play out on the small stage of the village; that was the price of being one of the vicar's daughters for the last thirty years. Everyone knew everything about her, sometimes even before she did.

She'd learned their family dog before Charlie, Molly, had died from a well-meaning neighbour expressing condolences as Esther had walked home from school. In her teenaged years, she'd discovered her sister Rachel had been dumped by her boyfriend by the woman at the post office shop. That was how life went in a village like Thornthwaite, and Esther had learned to live with it, mainly by never giving anyone anything to talk about it. Too bad that wasn't possible now.

"So." Ruth put down two Bakewell tarts, each on its own little plate with a napkin, on the table. "Is everything all right, Esther?"

Esther took a sip of tea, closing her eyes as she savoured the comforting warmth of the drink her mother believed cured almost every ailment, or at least helped a little. Unfortunately, she still felt empty and aching inside, and no amount of tea, lovingly brewed as it was, could help that. She didn't think anything could.

"I've left Will." Best to state it plainly, up front, get the worst right out and then try to recover. Soldier on, as she was desperate to do, mostly because she didn't know what else she *could* do. Most of her life had been about ploughing ahead, head down, chin tucked low, getting things done.

Ruth goggled at her, nearly spluttering her mouthful of tea. *"Left...* but..."

"We're separating," Esther clarified. "That's why I'm here. Will offered to be the one to leave, but with the farm it didn't make much sense." She put her hands flat on the table, her wedding ring winking in the light. She'd wondered about taking it off, making things clearer, at least in her own mind, but she didn't feel ready for that yet. She'd only been separated, informally at that, for two hours.

"Oh, Esther." Ruth bit her lip, looking near tears. "Is

this... is this because of the baby?"

"There was no baby, Mum," Esther reminded her. Even now, two months after the miscarriage—if she could even call it that—she felt the lightning flash of pain, like a toothache but in her heart. The blank blackness of the ultrasound screen still reverberated through her, an image she'd never be able to banish, an image of nothing, and she'd felt an awful nothingness when she'd seen it, and then something worse. Something she couldn't bear to articulate, even to herself, and certainly not to her mother.

"There was a baby, Esther," Ruth said quietly, her expression both sad and dignified. "It's just that it died very early."

"So it's in heaven?" Esther answered, unable to keep a sarcastic edge from entering her voice, and her mother winced. Esther felt a flash of guilt, on top of the pain. She hadn't meant to sound so cutting, so disbelieving, but she'd seen the screen and her mother hadn't. There had been nothing there. Absolutely nothing. And faith felt like a very frayed, thin thread indeed in moments like that one, although her parents chose to cling to it as often as they could.

"Sometimes this happens," the doctor had said, called in by the newly-qualified and nervous ultrasound technician. "The gestational sac is empty, because the embryo never actually developed..."

No embryo. No baby, and there never even had been. All along, while they'd been telling everyone and buying booties and baby gros, there had been nothing there. It felt like a mean trick played on them by fate—or God, if she wanted to believe the way her parents did, except of course they didn't believe God operated like that. No doubt, her father would smile sadly and say there was some wretched purpose in this, as there was in everything. Esther reached for her tea.

"All right," Ruth relented, her tone cautious. "As you say, then. But it's still a loss, Esther, no matter what showed up on that screen."

Esther buried her nose in her mug and kept her gaze lowered. No need to reply, then, although she still felt churlish, and she hated hurting her mother, who had to be one of the gentlest people on earth. How she shared the same DNA, Esther had no idea. She was certainly missing some of those crucial genes.

"Is that why you and Will have separated?" Ruth pressed, sounding genuinely upset. "Because grief can do strange things to people, Esther. Trust me, I know—"

"I know you know." Esther could hardly compare her own relatively paltry loss to her mother's grief over her only son and Esther's younger brother, Jamie, hit by a car and killed instantly when he was only ten years old. It had been twenty years ago, but sometimes the pain still felt fresh and raw, like a wound that kept breaking open, oozing blood, reminding everyone of how much it had hurt.

Over the years, they'd all become used to his absence, gaping as it was. They toasted him at Christmas and on his birthday in July, recalled happy memories, smiling and laughing a little, and occasionally brought out the photos. It all seemed healthy and right, the sort of thing you read about in self-help books as the proper way to manage grief, but sometimes Esther felt as if they were just applying a layer of gloss to an ugly stain. It didn't make it better. In some ways, it only made it worse.

Which was why, in her own blunt, forthright way, she'd decided to name this particular wound for what it was. Something that couldn't heal instantly or easily or maybe even at all. And it wasn't the miscarriage. It was her marriage.

"Do you mind if I stay here for a while?" she asked her mother.

"Oh, darling, of course not. We have the room, obviously, but..." Ruth trailed off, looking unhappy, and Esther knew why. She hated the thought of Esther and Will being apart, and she probably thought a romantic dinner out at The Winter Hare, the village's tiny bistro, would knock the problem on its head, bring them back together, easy peasy. All they needed was a little wine and good food to grease the wheels of their creaky marriage.

Unfortunately, life didn't work like that. And Will wouldn't even think of taking her out to dinner, not that Esther would want to go. They didn't have that kind of money, and they'd both see it as a waste.

"Thank you," Esther said briskly as she stood up from

the table. "And thanks for the tea. I should be getting on. I'm due for a farm visit out near Penrith in an hour."

"All right," Ruth said. She looked like she wanted to say something else, but Esther turned away, taking both of their mugs to the sink and rinsing them out. "Is Dad around?" she asked, mainly because she wanted to avoid him and the prospect of another concerned conversation, his well-meaning but prying questions, the commiserating clap on the shoulder.

"He's doing a funeral visit," Ruth said. "Mary Stanton died—do you remember her? She always sat in the back pew, wearing a pillbox hat." She smiled in fond, bittersweet recollection.

Esther vaguely remembered the woman; she'd stopped going to church when she'd moved back to Thornthwaite after uni, much to the quiet grief of her parents, and she only barely remembered the parade of grey-haired wrinklies who had, over the years, passed her sweets and pinched her cheek, told her how tall she was, how like her mother or father.

"That's too bad," she said as she dried her hands on the dish towel hung over the Aga's rail and then gave Charlie a pat as his tail thumped on the floor.

"She was ninety-three. She lived a good, long life."

"Yes, that's something I suppose." A silence ticked on, both of them lost, or perhaps trapped, in their own thoughts. Then Esther turned towards the door. "I'd better get on. I'll just take my suitcases upstairs." She paused. "Is there a bedroom you'd prefer that I…"

"You can have the one you used to share with Rachel," Ruth answered. "Or if you'd rather have a little privacy, one of the spare rooms on the top floor. Whatever you like, Esther, of course."

"Okay." Esther smiled, grateful for her mother's easy acceptance of her situation, even if she clearly didn't like it. "Thanks, Mum."

The house was quiet all around her, the only sound the steady ticking of the grandfather clock in the hall, as Esther hefted her two suitcases up the wide staircase. The vicarage had been built on grand proportions two hundred years ago, with soaring ceilings, sashed windows, and rooms the size of football pitches. It made the place freezing no matter what the season, with draughts regularly blowing through the old, thin windowpanes and heat rising to the high ceilings. Still it was lovely, and even now it felt like home. Perhaps it always would, even after her parents moved out in four months, when her father took up a pastor's position in China.

Esther paused outside her old room, which faced her parents' bedroom, and then decided to head up the narrow stairs to what had once been the old servants' quarters but now housed two cosy guestrooms under the eaves, mostly used when her parents had temporary lodgers—mercy guests, Rachel called them, for they never paid anything. Priests without posts, locals down on their luck, whatever waif or stray was currently in need of a bed and a roof over their head. And now that was her.

She chose the room on the right, with the small window that overlooked Lonscale Fell, now covered in a white, glittering frost even though it was March. She dumped the suitcases by the bed, unable to face unpacking just then. She also felt unable to face heading out to Penrith to visit Andrew Tyson and see how he was getting on with his drystone walls.

Her job at Natural England involved some travel to farms around the Lake District, encouraging farmers in their implementation of environmental programs and clean technology. It also involved many chats around the kitchen table and countless cups of tea. She was part civil servant, part counsellor—and sometimes she felt like the last person on earth who should be dispensing advice of any kind. She certainly felt that way now.

When Esther wasn't travelling to farms, she worked from home, part of a budget cut made in the last few years to reduce full-time office workers. Esther missed the camaraderie of the office in Penrith, and she disliked the ever-increasing mundane reality of the government box ticking and spreadsheet filling her job now required. Half her job, it seemed, was simply proving she was doing something. Still, it was the only job she'd ever known, and she believed in its mission wholeheartedly, which was what had kept her going this long.

With a sigh, she ran a brush through her unruly brown

hair before catching it up in a ponytail. She glanced in the little square mirror above the bureau; deeper crow's-feet by her hazel eyes, and stronger lines from nose to mouth. She was nearly thirty-six years old and showing her age. That had been what had spurred them to finally try for a baby. Those eggs were getting curdled, or whatever happened to unused eggs. Did they wither? Shrivel? *Explode?*

Downstairs, Ruth came out of the kitchen as Esther headed for the front door. "Will you be home for supper—"

Esther pictured her and her parents gathered around the kitchen table every night, suffering through tense, concerned silences as Ruth and Roger struggled to know what to say to their errant daughter. The one who had failed, who had had to limp home, downtrodden and depressed.

"I'm not sure," Esther hedged as she shrugged on her waxed jacket. "I'll ring you."

"All right." Ruth watched her go, clearly struggling not to say something Esther obviously didn't want to hear, and then with a distracted, apologetic smile aimed at her mum, Esther wrenched open the door and she was free.

The air was sharp and cold, with the bone-pervading damp that three weeks of wintry rain had caused, even though the sun was now attempting to break out from behind a bank of dark, dank clouds and spring was technically only a few weeks from now.

The air was still, the only sound the bleating of lambs in the distance. It was the middle of lambing season, and Esther had felt a curdling of guilt in her stomach that morning for leaving Will at the busiest time of a sheep farmer's year. But she hadn't felt as if she'd had any choice; it had been either that or claw her own eyes out.

Things between them had been getting steadily more strained, the silences that had once been comfortable and uncomplicated feeling like a scream that Esther struggled to suppress.

When she'd woken that morning she'd felt, with a leaden certainty, she couldn't wade through one more unendurable day. She just couldn't. And so, after breakfast, she'd told Will she'd thought they should separate. He'd stared at her blankly, as if she'd been speaking Swahili.

"Separate? What on earth are you talking about?"

"Oh, come on, Will." Esther dumped a frying pan in the sink and stared despairingly around at the cluttered mess of the low-ceilinged kitchen of Will's family home for nearly a hundred years. "Even you have got to realize things haven't been good between us."

"Even me? And what's that supposed to mean?" He was standing by the door, wearing an old fleece, mud-spattered all-weather trousers, and wool socks, a Wellington boot in one hand. His hair was an unruly shock of light brown around his weather-beaten face, his eyes, piercing blue, now narrowed.

Esther had always found Will's rugged, farmer looks sexy, but now he just seemed tired. It was six-thirty in the morning and he'd already been up for two hours.

"Nothing." She shook her head, too tired herself to go into lengthy explanations. And neither of them were the emotional sort, anyway. They didn't analyse each other's words or rake over old arguments. They didn't give each other lovey-dovey nicknames or send sappy love notes, never mind some kind of appalling sext. They just got on with things, two sensible people, happy in each other's company. Until now. Or, really, until the last few months, when Esther had gone into this awful, emotional tailspin. She was still trying to regain her balance, and feared she never would.

"Well, what are you talking about then, separating?" Will put his boot down. "I've got nowt time to have a pagger, Esther."

Esther always knew when Will's emotions were engaged, because he lapsed into the Cumbrian dialect he usually avoided, not wanting to seem parochial. Sheep farming was a gentleman's business these days; Oxford-educated philosophers were buying up farms in the fells and then writing blasted books about it. Will couldn't afford to seem like some sort of backwards yokel.

"I don't want to fight," Esther said. "I thought I was stating the obvious."

"It's not bloody obvious to me. Look, is this about the baby? Because—"

"It's not about the baby. That was just... a symptom, I suppose."

Will looked thunderous. "A *symptom?* Of what?"

"Of us not working anymore," Esther burst out. Of her not working, as a wife, as a person. "Of not being happy," she persisted, "either one of us, not really. Come on, Will. Tell me you haven't been miserable these last few weeks."

He stared at her, a storm in his eyes, and said nothing. That was answer enough, surely.

"I'll move back to the vicarage," Esther said. "It's the most sensible thing."

"If you feel you can't live with me," Will said, sounding furious, "then I'll be the one to move—"

"Will, come on." He had an old-fashioned code of gentlemanly behaviour, but it didn't make sense now. "You have the farm, and the lambs to see to. I'll go."

He stared at her, his jaw bunched and working, his eyes snapping icy blue sparks. "Fine."

"I'll leave this morning."

"Can't wait to get away, can you?"

Esther flinched but took it as her due. This was her fault. She accepted that. She should have been strong enough to keep muddling on, the same as always. She knew Will was. He would have gone on another forty years, the same day in and day out, without a flicker. She was the one who had suddenly detonated inside, ruining everything.

Will nodded tightly and then yanked on his boot. He paused in the doorway, slightly stooped under the low stone lintel, looking as if he wanted to say something, but wasn't sure what. And in the end, that had been part of the problem, hadn't it? They'd never known what to say to one another. It just hadn't mattered all that much until grief had reared up and sucker-punched them both.

Except you're not all that grief-stricken, are you?

That was a treacherous little voice she quickly silenced now. It was hard enough dealing with all the other rubbish she had going through her mind. Climbing into her beat-up Land Rover, she gripped the steering wheel and set her jaw, determined to soldier on, and not to think, to wonder, to doubt.

She couldn't picture her future—living at her parents' at thirty-five? Really? And besides, her mum and dad were moving out of the vicarage in just four short months. They were moving all the way to China, and that was something Esther tried not to think about, either.

She often acted as if she merely endured her parents' enthusiastic presence in her life, but the truth was, she couldn't imagine them not in it, the strong and silent foundation to everything she did and believed.

She couldn't imagine not being able to stop by the vicarage whenever the feeling took her, to sip tea and eat her mother's delicious baking while she tried—sometimes harder than others—not to roll her eyes on her mother's unsubtle poking and prying; the when-are-you-going-to-have-a-baby conversation had been dancing around that table for years.

The sudden sting of tears behind her lids took Esther by

surprise. She was so not a crier. She hadn't cried that morning, when she'd packed her bags in the eerily silent farmhouse, with Toby, Will's springer spaniel, twelve years old, a puppy when they had been dating, whining at the bottom of the old, narrow stairs he was no longer spry enough to climb, sensing something was wrong.

She hadn't cried when she'd seen that awful, blank screen at the hospital, *felt* the silence in a moment when she should have heard the watery whoosh of her baby's heartbeat. She hadn't even cried when her brother Jamie had died; she'd been called from her history classroom in Year Ten, taken to the head teacher's office, everyone looking far too solemn.

In each case, she'd just felt frozen inside, and the truth was, she'd never tested to see how deep or thick that layer of ice was, or whether any emotion lurked underneath. And now she was afraid to find out, afraid to probe those dark depths and discover how deep they went. Afraid she'd drown.

Eyes narrowed against the wintry glare of the sun emerging from behind the clouds, Esther drove over the little stone bridge that crossed St. John's Beck and out of Thornthwaite.

Chapter Two

WILL LANGLEY HAD always been a man of few words. He'd never minded, but now, when it was too late, he found words bubbling up inside him in a ferment of feeling, surprising and infuriating him because Esther had already left. He'd watched her Land Rover pull out of the farmyard, the hard-packed dirt glittering with frost, and then down the narrow, rutted track that led to the B-road into Thornthwaite, just over a mile away. She'd gone and bloody left him.

He still couldn't believe it. Couldn't accept it, even though he supposed he had to. And now it was too late to ask her to stop, *wait,* and then demand what on earth she was going on about, because as far as he was concerned this had come out of nowhere. Hadn't it?

He worked all day, spending most of it in the lambing shed, with two first-time ewes who were having difficult labours, as well as looking after a weak lamb who hadn't been able to feed from his mother. He'd docked a dozen lambs born in the last two days, the pockets of his trousers full of the rubber rings used to shorten their tails, his hands tinted a sickly yellow from iodine. The joys of lambing season.

At least the work kept him from thinking about Esther, although the knowledge of her departure, the sight of her looking so weary and resigned as she stood by the sink, was emblazoned onto his brain. Even when he was elbow-deep in an ewe he could still see it, the unfortunate movie screen in the back of his mind, his wife looking as if she couldn't stand another minute in his house, his life, as if she'd been beaten down by it all, by *him*. And he hadn't even realized.

At half past six, he stomped back into the farmhouse, ducking under the lintel as he shucked off his mud- and blood-spattered boots and trousers. The long, narrow kitchen was dark, the only sound the low, comforting rumble of the Aga. Dirty dishes were still piled in the sink, a pile of old post on the table. Toby came up to Will and whined, licking his hand; he hadn't been fed, and he was normally given his dinner at six, by Esther, after work, while Will was still out in the fields or barns.

It was probably chauvinistic and shallow to miss the creature comforts Esther had provided, but right then, mucky and muscles aching, Will did. He missed the sight of a cosy kitchen, with something simmering on top of the Aga, a hot bath already drawn upstairs in the claw-footed tub that was a century old. He missed Esther's smile and the brisk way she'd hand him a thick ceramic mug of tea, steeped so strong he could just about stand a spoon in it, before he'd even asked. He missed Esther.

Why on earth had she left? They'd been fine, hadn't they? He'd thought they'd been fine. Mostly fine, anyway. Not as bad as all that. All right, yes, the last few months had been a bit... difficult. But they'd just lost a baby, and of course that had to affect Esther. It had affected him. Even now his heart clutched as he remembered how the realization had thudded through him. No baby. No more picturing a little boy or girl, a bean of a baby that would fit in the curve of his arm. No more thoughts of a family, how they would finally be one properly, after so many years of waiting and wanting.

He hadn't talked to Esther about it, though, because they'd never been talkers, and he'd thought she wanted some space. He'd expected them to struggle through to the other side, find their balance again. He hadn't thought it had been that bad, but apparently it had. For Esther.

Will reached for the old, dented copper kettle on top of the stove and filled it up at the deep, farmhouse sink as he stared moodily out at the farmyard, now cloaked in a soft, purple twilight. The two ewes had safely delivered their lambs, and no others had shown signs of labour, so he might actually have an evening free for once.

If Esther were here, they'd open a bottle of wine and watch a DVD box set in the sitting room, with a fire in the wood stove crackling away merrily, her feet in his lap. Simple pleasures, but they'd been good enough for him. Although if he was honest, they hadn't done something like that in a long while.

No, with a free evening, Esther would be at the kitchen table, peering at her laptop as she filled out one of her wretched spreadsheets for work, an endless round of government box ticking, and Will might have tackled the farm's accounts, something he was forever putting off. Or he would have watched the telly by himself—football, maybe, or a mindless crime show.

They would have spent the entire evening apart, until bedtime, when Will would have checked on the animals and Esther would have taken Toby out and turned off the lights, maybe made up a couple of fleece-covered hot water bottles to take upstairs with them.

Then they would have gone up to the antique, oak bed Will's great-grandfather had bought his bride as a wedding present, and undressed for bed mostly in silence, although sometimes with the off comment about the farm or Esther's work; they'd never needed many words between them.

Then they would have climbed into bed and snuggled under the duvet, Esther's icy toes tucked up against Will's calves, a hot-water bottle tucked between them like a baby.

The baby. That was what this had to be about, no matter what Esther had said. What else could it be? They'd been happy before then. At least Will had been happy. Now he wondered if he'd ever actually known what Esther thought or felt. He certainly hadn't seen this coming, not ever, and the complete lack of knowledge, the utter shock he felt, rocked him more than a little.

With a sigh, he patted Toby's head and went to fill up the dog's bowl. The fridge was depressingly empty for Will's own dinner; Esther was the one who did the food shopping, she obviously hadn't for a few days. He found a heel of hardened cheddar cheese and the end of a loaf, and with a pint of Langdale bitter he called it a meal.

He'd just sat down at the table when headlights flashed across the window from the farmyard, and Toby set to barking as a Land Rover parked in front of the house. *Esther.* She was back. Daft woman, she regretted leaving him. Of course she did. With a sloppy grin spreading over his face, Will rose from the table, nearly tripping over Toby in his eager haste.

The knock at the door made him pause; wouldn't Esther just come in—or was she being absurdly formal, for some reason? He opened the door, the smile wiped off his face as he saw Dan Trenton, the local vet and fiancé of Esther's sister Rachel, standing there. Of course it wasn't Esther. Will was an idiot.

"Dan." He nodded his greeting. "What brings you here? All my ewes are fine and hardy."

Dan smiled. "Good to hear it. Lambing going well?"

"Two tricky births this morning, but it ended all right." Will stepped aside so Dan could come in; a light, needling rain was falling and the air was frigid. "What's going on with you?"

"I was over at the Whitford farm and I saw your lights. I thought I'd stop in."

He knew about Esther, then. Will appraised his future brother-in-law rather grimly, wondering how he'd found out. Had Esther told him? Had she told everyone? Or maybe Rachel had worked it out from Esther and then gone to Dan. Either way Will didn't like it much. His business was his business... and Esther's. The last thing he wanted now was to have Dan asking well-meaning questions, or worse, looking at Will with some kind of pity because he couldn't keep a wife.

"Well, then," he said, not meaning to be unfriendly, at least not exactly.

Dan smiled easily, as unruffled as always. "I wondered if you felt like a pint at The Bell?"

"The Bell?" The Queen's Sorrow was the pub for most of Thornthwaite; The Bell was for day labourers and lads on a pub crawl, intent only on getting drunk and maybe having a bust-up if they'd had too much.

"Why not?" Dan shrugged. "The Queen's Sorrow always seemed a bit posh to me, all that Barbour and Burberry makes my eyes cross."

Dan was posh, though, even though he'd been born and bred in Thornthwaite. He'd gone off to Cambridge for uni and come back sounding like a gentleman; he wore waxed jackets and Hunter boots and was interviewed by *Cumbrian Life*. He embodied the gentrified side of farming life that wasn't real, as far as Will was concerned. Will was a dying breed, a farmer born and raised, not a hobbyist who'd made his fortune in London and bought a farm for laughs with his pocket change.

"I've got the lambs," he said.

Dan raised his eyebrows. "I thought you said you'd delivered two ewes this morning?"

"Yes, but…" There was no good reason why he shouldn't spare an hour or two at The Bell, but Will resisted all the same. He didn't want Dan, kind as he was, prying into his business. He didn't want to talk about Esther, not when he didn't even know what was going on, not really. Not when he felt so bloody raw from it all.

At the same time, he didn't want to stay in this cold, dark, empty house. It felt as if all the light and life had been sucked from its thick stone walls when Esther had packed up and left. And he'd just opened his last pint of bitter.

"All right then," Will said with a nod. "Let me wash a bit of the sheep off me, and I'll meet you there."

"Excellent. Shall I order us some food as well?" Smiling, Dan spared a bemused glance for the sorry bit of bread and cheese on the table.

"Might as well," Will answered gruffly.

Fifteen minutes later he'd washed the worst of the mud and blood off him, although he still smelled like sheep—a mixture of wool, dirt, grass, and animal. He'd never get that smell off him, not during lambing season, at least.

He changed into a fresh flannel shirt and jeans, and then climbed in his own Land Rover, as beaten up as Esther's, and started down the bumpy track towards Thornthwaite.

The Bell looked comforting, its door thrown open, the interior lit up like a Christmas candle. Will parked on the side of steep, narrow Finkle Street, and strolled down towards the pub. He paused in front, his gaze travelling instinctively over the little stone bridge towards the village church with its square, squat Norman tower, and the darkened bulk of the vicarage beyond. He saw a light winking from his father-in-law's study window, but otherwise the vicarage looked dark and empty.

Was Esther there? What was she thinking? Feeling? Questions he'd never needed to ask before, never thought to ask. He didn't like asking them now, and he particularly didn't like not knowing the answers.

"Will." Dan called to him from a booth in the back as he came into the pub, shouldering his way through a press of slick-haired footballer lads who were making a bit of a ruckus.

"Busy in here for a Wednesday night," he remarked as he slid into the bench opposite Dan.

"West Lakes Football Club," Dan explained. "They come here after practice every Wednesday, or so the bartender, Sam, said."

"Right." Will picked up his pint of bitter. "Cheers. I'll get the next round."

"I probably shouldn't have more than one," Dan said regretfully. "Driving and work tomorrow."

Will nodded, wiping the foam from his upper lip. "Next time, then."

Dan nodded and they put down their pints, appraising each other. Will decided to break the silence first. "So you know about Esther, then."

Dan ducked his head. "Sorry, mate."

"It's all right." Will shrugged, acting as if it was all of little consequence, which was as daft as anything he could have done. What mattered more? He had a pain in his chest, the way he suspected a heart attack would feel, but he knew it wasn't. "You heard the crack from Rachel, I suppose?"

Dan nodded. "She saw Esther this afternoon, at the vicarage."

Will nodded and took another sip from his pint.

"I really am sorry," Dan said after a moment. "I know things have been tough..."

"Did you?" Will interjected abruptly, his voice harder than he'd meant it to be, that raw wound opening wider. "Because I'm not sure I did."

Dan looed startled. "I meant with the pregnancy... the miscarriage, you know..."

"Aye, that was hard." There was a tightening in his chest as he remembered Esther's toneless description of what had happened. He hadn't gone to the twelve-week ultrasound; she'd briskly told him he didn't need to, and with things busy as ever at the farm, he'd taken her at her word, which, now that he thought about it, seemed like a bloody stupid thing to do.

And so, it had meant he'd learned that their baby had never even been by Esther matter-of-factly recounting the events of her appointment as she sat at the kitchen table peeling potatoes. Will remembered the long, brown strips of peel, the pure white of the potato, the incongruity of it all. Death and dinner. He had barely been able to choke out "Oh, Esther" before she'd risen and gone to the Aga.

"Tea will be in half an hour," she'd said. "Why don't you have a bath beforehand?"

Will had stared at her, at a loss. Even he wasn't so clueless when it came to feelings that he realized this wasn't the right or normal response to a miscarriage. It wasn't the response he felt inside, but hell if he'd known what to say or do.

"That was hard," Will told Dan, "but it was two months ago, and Esther hasn't seemed..." He paused, trying to think how Esther had seemed. As brisk as ever, surely, and maybe a little remote. But not grief-stricken. Not heartbroken. "Truth be told," he said, "Esther didn't seem as upset as all that." He looked down into his beer, feeling disloyal for saying such a thing, even if it was true. "At least on the surface, I mean." And he didn't really look much farther than that. He wasn't sure he knew how, not when what was on the surface had made him happy.

"Sometimes these things fester though, don't they?" Dan said, and Will stared at him blankly. Fester? Open sores on a hoof festered. Not feelings. And yet even he knew what Dan meant. A bit.

"Esther isn't the sort to hold a grudge or anything like that," he protested. "If she's got a problem, she'll tell you. Tell me." At least he'd thought she would—and she certainly had today. Except he still didn't feel any the wiser.

"True enough, I suppose," Dan acknowledged with a wry smile. "She can certainly be blunt, can't she? I got my hair cut a few weeks ago and she said it made me look like a shorn sheep." Will smiled a little; he'd never minded the sharp side of Esther's tongue. "But what do you think is going on, then?"

Will shrugged again. What else could he do? He had no idea what was going on, and even if he did, he didn't think he wanted to share it with Dan. But he did know his wife, or at least he'd thought he did, and she was one of the most practical, down-to-earth, no-nonsense people he knew, and so this kind of over-the-top, abrupt, and emotional behaviour was totally unlike her. That's what he couldn't get his head around.

Her practical, purposeful air had been one of the things that had attracted him to her, when they'd met ten years ago at a quiz night at The Queen's Sorrow. He'd looked at her and thought, *there's a woman who will tell you like it is. Who won't mess you about. A woman you could build a life, a family, with.* And then she'd laughed—a surprisingly deep, throaty, sexy sound, and Will had been sold.

He'd asked her out that night, they'd had dinner at a little Italian place in Keswick that weekend, and they'd been an item by Monday, engaged two years later, married the year after that. All smooth, smooth sailing, not a ripple in the water. Or so he'd thought. Now he had the uncomfortable sensation of feeling the need to question everything, *doubt* everything, something he never thought—or wanted—to do.

"Shall we order our food?" he asked, and Dan nodded. "I'll go up to the bar. What would you like?"

"Fish pie for me, thanks."

Will nodded and rose from his seat, grateful to have a short reprieve from Dan's kind but cack-handed attempt at a man-to-man chat.

He shouldered his way to the bar; the football lads were getting a bit arsey, on their third or fourth pints by now, the raucous laughter holding a slightly menacing edge. Will leaned his forearms on the bar and gave his order to the hassled-looking barman, who was keeping an eye on the lads behind him.

"Busy tonight, eh, Sam?" Will asked.

Sam had gone to the comp with him and taken over the pub five years ago, after it had been run nearly into the ground by a bickering couple constantly on the brink of divorce. Not like him and Esther… or so he'd thought.

"A wee bit too busy, I'm thinking," Sam answered. "Those lads need nowt more to drink. They're well kaleyed. What are you having then, Will?"

Will gave the food order, and then waited while Sam rang it up on the till. He glanced to the man parked on a stool to the right of him, an old codger with a flat cap pulled down low over his face, his expression set and stony, his gnarled hands clasping his pint of ale.

That could be him in another thirty years, Will realized with a jolt. Coming to the pub every night for the company, never mind the beer. Living alone, with only a dog to ease his loneliness, the kind of fate he'd feared until he'd met Esther. Until he'd found a place with her, a *home,* damn it. He didn't want to give that up without a fight. He couldn't.

Staring at the old geezer next to him with his surly, set expression, he had a sudden urge, almost a compulsion, to walk out of the pub, right up to the vicarage, and take Esther by the shoulders and ask her to come home. Demand or beg, he didn't much care which at this point. He just wanted her back.

"That'll be sixteen fifty, Will."

Will glanced up at Sam and nodded, his mind still on the man next to him, on the unending road of loneliness stretching in front of him, and on Esther. Always on Esther. He handed over a twenty-pound note, and as he did so the man on the stool glanced over.

"Areet, eh?" he asked in a Cumbrian accent so thick even Will struggled to understand it.

"Areet," he answered brusquely, not quite meeting his eye, and then he took his change and headed back to his table.

Dan seemed to have taken the hint that Will wasn't up for some kind of heart-to-heart chat, and so they talked about farming and football for the rest of the evening, and after another half-pint—since he was driving—Will managed to relax a little.

"It'll come all right," Dan said as they walked out of the pub; Sam was in the process of forcibly ejecting the drunk lads, taking two by the scruffs of their necks.

"What will come all right?" Will asked as he stepped out onto the pavement. The night was black and starless, the air damp and chill, full of the plaintive sound of bleating sheep, the symphony of farming life.

"You and Esther."

"Ah." It all came back to him with a chest-slamming thud, nearly making him take a step back into the two lads who were keyed up and drunk and no doubt looking for a fight. And Will almost thought about giving it to them, just to relieve the pressure building inside him, pressure that had nowhere to go.

"What are you staring at?" one of the lads asked rudely, his fists balling at his sides. He reeked of beer and cheap aftershave, dressed in a tight football jersey and a pair of low-slung trackie bottoms.

"What do you care, what I'm staring at?" Will growled back. He was six inches taller and at least two stone heavier.

"Hey, hey, let's not get worked up here," Dan said easily, and with a hand on his shoulder he steered Will towards the street. "Don't waste your breath on those lads, mate."

"Yeah, yeah." Will unclenched his fists and flexed his fingers. He wasn't a fighter. He'd only swung a punch once in his life, and he'd lived to regret it more than just about anything he'd done. But that was something he didn't think about, a memory he'd dropped into the deep, empty well inside his mind. He never looked down there.

But right now he was angry, and he wasn't used to it, and he didn't know where to put it. Why the *hell* had Esther left him?

He swung away from The Bell and started down the pavement, only to come to a stop when he saw the two figures on the other side of the street, both of them standing stock still, looking shocked. Dan's fiancée Rachel… and Esther.

Chapter Three

ESTHER STOPPED RIGHT there in the street and stared at Will as if she hadn't seen him in ten years, rather than ten hours. His hair was rumpled, sticking up on one end, as if he'd driven his fingers through it or forgot to use a comb all day—or both. He was staring at her the way she suspected she was staring, mouth open, eyes wide. Gormless.

"Oh…" Next to her Rachel muttered under her breath, and Esther glanced at her sister sharply as she clocked that Will was with Dan, and she was with Rachel, all of them out at the pub, albeit different ones. *Something is rotten in the state of Denmark, or rather Thornthwaite.*

"Did you plan this?" Esther asked in a low voice, and Rachel bit her lip.

"Not… exactly…"

Yeah, right. Esther felt as if she was about thirteen, being pushed forward by a giggly friend to give a boy her phone number. Except Will wasn't standing there waiting, trying to look cool. No, he'd actually walked on, Dan hurrying to catch up, right around the corner to Finkle Street, out of view.

"Good thing, then," Esther said as briskly as she could, and marched on towards the vicarage, trying not to feel hurt. It had been a bad idea to come out with Rachel, anyway. She'd only agreed because her sister was a cross between a golden retriever and a pit bull when it came to social occasions—jumpy, overfriendly, and aggravatingly tenacious. And Esther had been feeling the littlest bit lonely, just hours into her newfound separation.

"Esther, wait," Rachel called, and hurried to catch up with her.

Esther broke her stride, but only just. "Tell me the truth," she demanded as they crossed the little stone bridge over St. John's Beck. "Did you plan that?"

"We didn't plan it," Rachel hedged, but the 'we' gave it away.

"So, let me guess. After I told you that I'd left Will, you and Dan decided to hatch this cute little plot to take us both out to the pub, and then, oh, wow, what a coincidence, we meet outside in the street, fall into each other's arms, and boom, we're back together." Esther shook her head, trying to dissolve the hard lump of disappointment and anger that had formed at the back of her throat. Why had she become so stupidly emotional? Why did this hurt so much?

"It wasn't quite like that," Rachel said as they turned up the darkened lane to the church and the vicarage beyond. "We just wanted to help. Give you both someone to talk to.

Honestly, Esther, that was all."

Esther sagged, knowing she was being prickly, even for her. It was just that she felt so lamentably raw. "I know," she said on a gusty, ragged sigh. "I know you mean well, Rachel. It's just… I'm not there yet, okay? Neither of us are. This is… very new."

"Sorry," Rachel whispered, looking so wretched Esther took pity on her.

"You don't need to apologize. You took me out for a drink, and I was in desperate need of a large glass of wine."

"That's the least I could do." Rachel gave her sister a rather shaky smile. "Because, Esther, if you and Will don't make it… is there any hope for the rest of us?"

Esther stopped where she was and turned slowly towards Rachel. "What do you mean by that?"

"Just that you guys always seemed so solid. Perfect for each other, low maintenance, comfortable, just happy to *be*, you know? And if that isn't working after all…" Rachel trailed off, biting her lip.

"You don't need to worry about you and Dan. What happened between Will and me… well, it's not a problem you're likely to have." A pressure was building in her chest. Rachel would never react the way Esther had to life's tragedies. No one would, because it wasn't normal, to feel the way she had. Still did.

Rachel frowned. "What did happen?" she asked gently, but Esther just shook her head.

"I can't go into that now. I've got to be up at six tomorrow to drive to a farm north of Carlisle. And… and I just can't. I'll see you later." She started walking again, quickly, her head down, the misery in her chest swamping and suffocating her. She hated feeling like this, but she didn't have the energy to fight her way through the morass. Who knew what was on the other side, anyway?

Rachel got into her car, which she'd parked in front of the vicarage, as Esther stepped into the house. Inside everything was quiet; her father was at a wardens' meeting and Ruth was curled up on a sofa in the upstairs family room, Charlie stretched out by the fire, as she watched one of the BBC dramas she liked.

"Everything all right?" she asked lightly when Esther dutifully poked her head in the doorway, feeling like a teenager reporting in before curfew.

"Fine. I'm just shattered, and I've an early morning. Good night, Mum. And… thanks." Ruth smiled and nodded, her eyes seeming sad, and Esther turned away, towards the upstairs.

Her room was freezing, due to the lack of central heating on the vicarage's top floor, although her mother had thoughtfully brought up a space heater for her, as well as a hot-water bottle.

Esther stared at the fleece-covered rubber bottle and the lump in her throat thickened. That bottle made her think of those wintry nights with Will, tucked up in bed, happy simply to be, just as Rachel had said. They had had something, Esther knew that. It just hadn't been enough. *She* hadn't been. She couldn't have been, to feel this way now.

Esther got ready for bed, slipping beneath the cold sheets, clutching her hot-water bottle. The space heater emitted a feeble, electric warmth that barely took the chill from the air.

She closed her eyes, willing sleep to come, but despite her exhaustion everything in her felt wide awake and aching. The house seemed unfamiliar even though she'd grown up in it, and the creaks and rattles as the wind battered the window-panes and the house settled into itself kept making her jolt awake. Eventually she fell into an uneasy sleep, only to surface from sleep at four-thirty in the morning as if she were coming from deep underwater.

She showered and dressed, stumbling around in the dark, and then drank a cup of instant coffee by the Aga while Charlie lifted his head, looking at her in vague resentment for disturbing his slumber.

By the time she hit the road a little after five she was feeling awake but grotty, as if it was the end of a long day rather than the beginning.

The rambling sheep farm near Hexham was a pleasant spot, at least, and the drive up the A595 was smooth and uneventful, save for a few tractors.

As Esther pulled into the farmyard, a couple of spaniels set to barking, and the front door opened before she'd got out of the car. Jane Telford stood on the stone slab step, her hands on her hips, a smile on her broad face.

"I've got a brew on," she called, and then whistled for the dogs, who, after sniffing Esther thoroughly, retreated to the kitchen. Esther had always liked the Telfords' farmhouse. She only visited twice a year, but the family always welcomed her like a long-lost and much-loved relative. Their farmhouse was similar to hers and Will's—or was it just Will's now?—except there were more people and dogs, and somehow that made the place feel more loved and lived in, a proper home, than the empty rooms of her own house, rooms they'd expected to fill eventually. At least Will had.

Esther ducked her head under the stone lintel as she stepped into the cheerful kitchen; the kettle was whistling away on top of a dark blue Rayburn, and the dogs were getting under everyone's feet, tails wagging furiously.

"You'll have a cuppa," Jane said, not a question, and Esther nodded. She had so many cups of tea during a day of farm visits that by evening she could practically hear her insides slosh. "You'll never guess who's here," Jane continued as she poured boiling water from the kettle into an enormous brown teapot that looked as if it had come over on the ark. "Izzy," she finished triumphantly, as if that should mean something to Esther.

Slightly panicked, she scrolled through her mental Rolodex of names, trying to recall an Izzy. Izzy... Izzy Telford... ah, yes, Jane and Jim's oldest daughter, who had married two years ago. Esther had been invited to the wedding, a big local knees-up in the village pub, but she hadn't gone, she couldn't remember why not now. Probably because of the farm. That was usually why she didn't do anything.

"How is Izzy?" she asked as she sat down at the kitchen table and a dog flopped onto her feet. "And... Darren?" The name popped unbidden out of her mouth and she hoped she'd got it right.

"They're right as rain," Jane answered, handing Esther a mug of tea. "And Izzy's had a bairn since you've been here last!"

"A bairn..."

"A wee one," Izzy said with a laugh, coming into the kitchen in her dressing gown, unselfconsciously sporting a serious case of bedhead, a newborn baby nestled in her arms, its fists curled up by her face like two flowers, the gently pursed lips reminding Esther of a rosebud.

"Born just three weeks ago," Jane said proudly. "And doing so well. Isn't she, precious?" She leaned over to give the baby a smacking kiss on the forehead.

"Adorable," Esther murmured. She was struggling to put a smile into place. "A girl?" she added, just to check, because you never knew.

Izzy laughed. "She certainly is. Caitlin Rose."

"Lovely."

"Why don't you have a cuddle, then?" Jane suggested

and when Esther opened her mouth to politely say she'd rather not—although how she would phrase that, she wasn't sure—Jane just let out a bellow of laughter and nodded at Izzy to bring the baby forward. "Go on, then. You'll be needing some practice, won't you?"

Esther froze. "Practice..."

"Well, you'll be having the bairns soon enough, won't you?" Jane said as she settled herself at the end of the table with her own mug of tea.

"Mum," Izzy said with an embarrassed laugh, "don't be so nosy."

"Nosy? Eh?" Jane looked startled and a bit offended. "I'm just being friendly like. Esther and I go back, don't we, love? Ten years, isn't it now, that you've been working for Natural England?"

"Eleven," Esther replied with a small smile. Then Izzy tipped the baby into her arms like a barrow full of dirt and she jolted forward, anxious to keep the tiny person safe. Because it was a person, this little bundle in her arms, which was such an amazing thing. Esther adjusted her hold on the baby, making sure she was supporting her head.

She hadn't held many babies in her life but she knew that much at least. Before the miscarriage, she'd read at least half of *What to Expect When You're Expecting*, a book that had alarmed more than comforted her. There had been so much she needed to know, so many things that could go wrong. Although, in the end, it had turned out she hadn't needed to know much at all.

"You've got the hang of it now," Jane said approvingly. "A natural, you are."

Esther let out a dry little laugh. A natural she was not. Not by a million, zillion miles.

"She's lovely," she told Izzy, who was watching her in concern, sensing, clearly, that something wasn't quite right. It had to be obvious. "Really lovely." She jiggled the sleeping baby a little, studying the faint blond eyebrows and lashes, the perfect, rosy skin, the full, round cheeks and pouty lips. Then she held the baby out to be taken, and Izzy scooped her up, a professional after just three weeks.

Would she have been like that, confident and laidback with this tiny person entrusted to her care? Esther had no idea. Part of the problem had been that she hadn't been able to imagine herself pregnant or as a mother, not really. She couldn't picture herself with a big, proud baby bump, or holding a mewling infant to her breast. Not at all.

So when that blank, black screen had come into focus, and the doctor had explained about the baby-who-wasn't, part of her hadn't even been surprised. And part of her had been... but, no. She couldn't think about that. And she couldn't possibly explain it to Will, not that he'd ever even thought to ask.

"Right," Esther said as she hurried to finish her cup of tea. "How's Jim getting on with the Environmental Steward-ship Scheme, then?"

Two hours later she was climbing back into her Land Rover, having walked with Jim Telford through his fields that were currently not being used for agricultural management, and listened to his litany of complaints about the price of feed, the terrible weather, and the government's endless interference. All said good-naturedly, of course, while Esther nodded and murmured and soothed, and then reminded him of what still needed to happen if he wanted to be part of the environmental scheme.

Another farm visit later, the last for a few weeks, she was heading back home to do the endless paperwork and data entry that working for a government agency required. Dusk was falling as she drove along the A595, now in slow-moving traffic as opposed to the peaceful quiet of that morning. She ached with tiredness, driving on autopilot, so much so that she hadn't realized what she'd done until she'd pulled into the farmyard and turned off the car. Will came to the kitchen door, frowning out into the dusky evening as she started to get out. Far too late, Esther realized her mistake.

"Esther?" He sounded disbelieving, and no wonder. She'd left him yesterday, and here she was back again. "What are you doing here?"

"I..." She thought about blustering her way through some credible reason—she'd forgotten some clothes or papers or something—but she was too tired to think of anything and her mind blanked. Will stared. "I was driving from Carlisle and I came here automatically," she confessed.

"Sorry." She turned back to the car, utterly dispirited at the thought of getting in and driving to the vicarage, yet knowing that was what she needed to do.

"Wait." Will barked the word, then took a deep breath and let it out slowly. "Since you're here, don't you think we should at least talk?"

"We never talk, Will."

"Fair enough, but how about we start now? Because I still haven't got a clue as to why you left me the way you did and, frankly, I'd like to know." He sounded belligerent, even angry, and Esther didn't think she had the energy or strength to deal with Will in that mode, not that he got in it all that often. In fact, basically never.

"I don't know if now's really a good time..."

"I've put some sausages in the oven," he persisted, and then gave her one of his old, wry smiles. "Sorry, it's the best I could do for dinner, but, please, stay. Tell me something, because I'm in the dark, Esther, and I don't even know what words to say." He stared at her, his expression steady and strong, reminding Esther of why she'd fallen in love with him all those years ago.

Because she had fallen in love, hadn't she? They hadn't married simply because it made sense or seemed comfortable, surely? It was a question that had been rattling around in her brain—and in her heart—for a while now and she still didn't know how to answer it. But Will deserved some answers, even if she doubted they'd satisfy him. She certainly couldn't tell him the truth. At least not all of it.

"All right," she relented and closed the car door. "I am a bit hungry."

She followed him into the kitchen, blinking at how much a mess a man could make in one day. Grease and sauce-splattered dishes were piled up in the sink, and a load of dirty washing had made it from upstairs to the vicinity of the washer, if not actually in it. There was an overpowering smell, more so than usual, of wet dog and sheep.

"Sorry," Will muttered. "I haven't…"

"I know it's lambing season." She moved aside a pile of post from a chair and sat down. "How have things been?"

"Two ewes delivered yesterday, another two this afternoon. They're all doing well."

"Good."

He rubbed the back of his neck, blinking at her in the dim light of the kitchen, with its thick stone walls and small, square windows. It was a cosy room when it was clean; for a second Esther thought of the Telfords' welcoming kitchen, little Caitlin in her arms. How different things might have been.

"What happened, Esther?" Will asked, the question bursting from him. "Just tell me straight. Why did you wake up yesterday morning and decide to leave me?"

"It wasn't like that, Will."

"I know it wasn't. It couldn't have been." With a sigh, he sank onto a chair opposite her, his elbows resting on the table. He was wearing an old Aran jumper that had more holes than not. Esther had got him a new one for his birthday a few months ago, but he kept saving it for special occasions, of which there hadn't been any. "It's only that it felt that way to me."

"Didn't you feel like something was wrong?" Esther asked quietly. "Because I felt it, not just in me, but between us." Like the fact, for example, that they hadn't had sex since before Christmas. Their sex life had always been enjoyable if a tiny bit predictable, but what married couple's wasn't? But she'd missed that kind of intimacy, where no words were needed at all.

"I suppose I could see that you weren't yourself," Will said slowly. "And I wasn't, either. But we lost a baby, Esther. That's a big thing. It takes time to recover."

She drew a breath and let it out slowly. "Does it?"

Will blinked at her. "What does that mean?"

"I don't know." She backtracked, not ready or willing to go into that whole mess of feeling, or lack of it. "Only, it wasn't just the pregnancy, Will, or losing it." That had been the trigger, maybe, but *only* the trigger. "It was everything," she said. "The way we never talk, and then the way something terrible can happen and neither of us have the words to deal with it. We just carried on, like life was normal and uncomplicated. We *always* just carry on." The bitterness spiking her words was evident to both. She sounded positively venomous, and even she was surprised at the depth of her emotion. But of course she wasn't telling him everything. She was acting as if they were the problem, when deep down she was.

Will was silent, staring at her, having no words. As usual. She stared back, full of despair, because she didn't even know what she wanted from this man, and worse, she couldn't confess the dark stew of feelings inside her—guilt and grief, sorrow and, worst of all, a deep, treacherous relief.

No wonder they didn't have any words. How on earth was she supposed to talk about *that?*

Chapter Four

WHAT HAD HAPPENED to his practical, sensible, no-nonsense wife? Esther was looking at him with a face full of sadness and Will had no idea what to say. He'd failed her somehow, he could see that, but damned if he knew what he should have done—or what to do now.

What he did know was that he hated feeling this way, like it was all up to him but he couldn't keep from getting it wrong. The way he'd felt with David, ten years ago, right in this kitchen.

Go on, then.

Three little words he would do anything to take back, but of course he couldn't.

"What would help?" he asked at last. "Counselling…" The word came with a bit of a shudder, because, in truth, he couldn't think of anything worse than sitting around and talking about his feelings with some sanctimonious stranger. But he would do it if it helped. At least he'd try.

"No, not counselling." Esther shared his shudder, she felt the same. They weren't as different as all that, no matter what Esther was saying or feeling now. But she obviously wanted something from him, something she wasn't getting, and the truth was, he didn't know if he could give it to her.

"All right, then. Let's talk right here and now." He took a deep breath, laid his hands flat on the old, scarred oak trestle table. "About the baby."

Esther looked away, her lashes sweeping downwards so he couldn't make out her expression at all. "I don't want to talk about the baby. There wasn't even a baby, anyway."

"Then what?" Will exploded. So much for his resolutions to be measured and reasonable. He hadn't felt this angry since... but, no. He needed to focus on Esther. "What do you want from me, then?"

"Nothing."

"Nothing? So you leave me and there's nothing I can do? And you still haven't given me a good reason, or any reason?" It was so bloody unfair. He felt powerless and he hated it.

"The reason is I couldn't take any more," Esther burst out. Will, having half-risen from his seat, sat back down with a thud. "I couldn't live like this for one more day, soldiering through, on and on, eating and sleeping together, and just living, with nothing else going on at all." She let out another shudder, this one going through her whole body, as she looked away.

"You sound like you need a holiday," Will ventured.

"No, not a holiday, because that would just be more of the same, except maybe on a beach somewhere." She shook her head as she gave a tired laugh. "Not that we ever went on many, or any, holidays."

He prickled; he couldn't help it. "It's hard with the farm."

"I know it is." She looked back at him with weary resignation. "It's just us, Will. The way we are. The way we've always been. I thought it was enough, just rubbing along together, but it isn't. Losing the baby made me realize that. Made me realize I couldn't do this anymore. I couldn't be the person I thought I was anymore." She said each sentence with a certain leaden resolve, as if she'd rehearsed the words. Lines in a play, one in which he had no wish to have a role. She didn't look at him as she said it, and he didn't know whether to believe her. Did she believe herself?

"So that's it?" he finally said, still scarcely able to believe it had come to this, and so quickly. "You're just... done?"

She hesitated, and he saw the torment in her eyes, felt it in himself. Marriages didn't end like this, did they? Not his. Not theirs. Seven years ago now, nearly eight, they'd stood in front of her father's church, holding hands and making vows that meant something. They'd eaten cake and drunk champagne in the vicarage garden with half the village in attendance, big, fat honeybees buzzing around the wisteria, a perfect, golden day in July.

He'd felt happier than he could ever remember feeling, at least since his parents had died when he was nineteen and the weight of the world had descended right onto his shoulders, a weight he'd bowed and eventually collapsed under.

With Esther, he'd finally felt it start to lift. Felt himself become whole again. He'd seen a future, and he'd *liked* it, damn it. He'd liked it a lot. So how had they ended up here?

"I don't give up that easily, Esther," he said, and it sounded like a warning. "Not just on your say so."

"What are you going to do, then?" She just sounded tired, and that stung. But what *was* he going to do? He had no idea. How did he make someone try? How did he get her to love him? The fact that it would have to be an effort hurt, and it felt wrong. Surely it wasn't supposed to work like that. It had never before, but perhaps it should have.

Esther glanced down at the pile of old post she'd removed from her chair and then sucked in a surprised breath. Startled, Will glanced at it too, and it took a few seconds for him to register the heavy, expensive-looking stationery of the wedding invitation on top. Esther's friend Helen from Natural England, getting married in a couple of weeks.

She lived in Newcastle now, and they'd RSVPed to the wedding at least a month ago. Will had organized coverage for the farm, which wasn't easy this time of year, but he'd known the wedding was important. Helen had been one of Esther's best friends, when she'd lived nearby in Penrith.

"When is that wedding?" he asked gruffly.

Esther didn't take her eyes from the invitation as she answered slowly, "Next weekend."

Will sat back in his seat and closed his eyes. "You're still going to go?"

"Yes..." The word came out uncertainly, and Will snapped his eyes open. "And what about me?" He liked Helen, and he'd got along with her fiancé Nathan, the few times they'd met. Now he wondered if Esther was going to bar him from going.

"Do you want to go?" She sounded incredulous.

"Why not?" Normally Will would probably make an excuse for ducking out of a party or event, especially if it was going to take the whole weekend. He wasn't the most social person out there, heaven knew, and the farm demanded all his attention and time.

But now? When this might be the only chance he had to spend time with his wife, and figure out what his next steps were, if he even had any?

"Yeah," he said firmly. "I'd still like to go."

"You would?" She sounded so surprised and Will couldn't really blame her. This was entirely out of his character.

"Makes it easier, doesn't it?" he persisted. "Awkward explaining, otherwise."

"You mean about us."

"I don't know about you, but I'm not ready to go bleating to the world that we've separated. Not until..." He paused, scanning her tired face, the sadness in her eyes. "Not until I understand a bit more about what's going on, at least."

Esther sighed, and then she nodded slowly. "I suppose you're right. It would be difficult to explain, and I don't want to take away from Helen's day."

"So we'll both go?"

"We might as well." Esther sounded both resigned and reluctant. "We've already booked the hotel."

"Have we?"

"Yes, I booked a hotel in the city," she answered a bit tartly. Should he have known? Should he have done it himself? "But it's not really appropriate now, staying in a place like that."

"I think we can share a bed without ripping each other's clothes off," Will retorted, "if that's what you mean."

"I'm not afraid of that," Esther shot back. "That's what we've been doing for the last six months."

He stared at her, gobsmacked. "Now what's that supposed to mean?"

"I'd say it was obvious," Esther retorted, leaving Will with no idea how to reply.

»»»«««

WILL STARED AT her for a few seconds, looking both baffled and furious, and Esther wondered if he even realized what she meant. If he'd noticed that deficit in their marital life. They certainly hadn't talked about it; they'd simply gone to bed each night, rolling over on to opposite sides, by silent, mutual agreement.

Before either of them could say anything more, the whiff of burning meat caught both their noses, and Will rose from his seat.

"Damn, the sausages." He opened the door of the Aga and a cloud of black smoke billowed out. "Sorry."

"It's fine." Esther rose, as well. "I wasn't that hungry, anyway." She'd lost her appetite.

"Esther..." Will stared at her, clearly frustrated, and she wished, bizarrely, that she could make it easier for him. Easier for them. But that would involve coming clean with how she really felt, how little she felt, and she wasn't ready for that. She wasn't ready for Will to hate her.

"I should go."

"Why don't we drive together on Friday, for the wedding?"

Two hours in the car. Esther supposed she could face that. They never talked in the car, anyway, and she didn't see that changing now.

"Fine." She stepped over Toby, who had sprawled hopefully by her feet and whined as she left. Her heart gave a little twist of sad longing. She'd known him since he was little more than a puppy, and she missed him now. "Bye, Tobes," she murmured, and stroked his silky head. He wagged his tail hopefully, his droopy eyes looking sad. Will stood by the sink, arms folded, face stony. Esther took a deep breath and kept walking.

As she drove down the narrow road towards Thornthwaite, she realized she couldn't face going back to the vicarage and her parents' endless, quiet concern. They meant well, they did, but at thirty-five it was hard to face that kind of worried attention over the dinner table every evening, not that she had yet. Still, she'd have to brace herself for it, evening after evening. But not tonight.

So, on the spur of the moment, Esther turned right before the bridge and went down a narrow lane of old tied cottages that had once belonged to the manor farm just outside the village, now a posh weekend residence for a London couple. Rachel's cottage was the last one, with a rusted iron gate and a garden that led into a watery ditch. Esther stepped over a clump of nettles as she made her way to the front door. Rachel had bought the cottage a few years ago, a fixer-upper that she hadn't yet found the time to fix up.

Now, Rachel and Dan were planning to sell both of their properties—Dan lived in a barn conversion a mile out of town—and buy their dream house. Catch Rachel at any odd moments, and she'd be sighing happily at visions of domestic bliss, all creamy Agas and quarry tiles, on Rightmove.

Esther knocked on the front door, already half-regretting her impulse. She loved her sister but Rachel was so full on, and she'd take Esther coming to her house as a sign that she wanted to have a big emotional sob-fest, which most definitely did not. A drink at the pub, with Rachel wide-eyed and well-meaning, had been hard enough.

"Esther." Rachel stared at her for a moment, clearly surprised, before she stepped aside. "Is everything okay? I mean, besides what's already…"

"I know what you mean." Esther stepped into the cluttered hallway. Rachel's house was just as messy as hers and Will's, but in an entirely different, and completely feminine, way. Tattered paperbacks, mainly romances and chick lit, were stacked in tottering piles in the tiny hallway, and the walls were crammed with dusty, framed posters of musicals Rachel had seen or been in during her university days, when she'd been part of an am-dram society.

Dried flowers—she saved just about every bouquet she'd ever been given or bought herself—were stuck in various vases or wine bottles, perched on windowsills or bookshelves. And clothes… clothes were everywhere. Sweaters, coats, scarves, dresses, and skirts. Rachel was the kind of person who tried on three outfits every morning before deciding on one, and left them all around the house, lying where they had been discarded.

"Sorry, if I'd known you were coming, I would have tidied up," Rachel muttered as she liberated a sofa cushion from two sweaters and a pair of high heeled boots.

"You never tidy up," Esther returned, trying to sound light and, as usual, not quite managing it. Why did she always have to be so stern?

"True enough, I suppose. Do you want a cuppa? Or

something stronger?"

"I don't even know." Esther sank onto the sofa and leaned her head back. "I just couldn't face going back to the vicarage. Mum and Dad are lovely, but..." She sighed. "There's only so much concern you can take."

"Duly noted. I won't ask a thing. I was just heating up a curry, if you want some."

Rachel was notorious for never cooking. She'd once boiled a pan of water and let it all evaporate, not noticing until the pan was blackened and the kitchen full of smoke. None of her sisters, of course, let her forget it. "That sounds lovely, thanks." Rachel went into the kitchen and Esther closed her eyes, a wave of tiredness crashing over her. She could practically fall asleep right there, and she thought she might have when she was prodded awake by Rachel holding a large glass of red wine.

"Thought we might as well. And here's the curry." She proffered two plates that smelled heavenly. "Tikka masala or chicken korma?"

"Korma, please." Esther straightened, rubbing her hands over her face. "You're a star, Rach, thanks."

Her sister made a funny face as she sank onto the sofa opposite with her own glass of wine and plate of curry. "It's not much."

"It is." Esther and Rachel hadn't been all that close in recent years. They hadn't been distant, either. They'd just... been. A lot of her life had become like that, Esther realized as she took a rather large sip of velvety-smooth wine. She'd just been going through the motions, the days, on and on, ploughing through until tragedy had jolted her awake. And, in truth, part of her wished she could retreat back into mindless hibernation, the busyness of merely doing.

"So, is it very difficult, being back with Mum and Dad?" Rachel asked after they'd eaten their curries in silence for a few minutes.

"I wouldn't actually know. I haven't spent all that much time there." Esther grimaced. "I'm avoiding them, to be honest, because I know how worried they are about me. They're not difficult, not like that. They just care so much." And sometimes that hurt, especially when she was feeling so wretched inside.

"We all care," Rachel said quietly, a hint of a smile in her eyes. "That's the thing with family. We just don't stop."

Esther managed a wry smile back. "I know, and I appreciate it, really. Deep down inside."

"Deep, deep down inside."

Esther let out a little huff of laughter. "Exactly. Why don't we talk about something a bit more cheerful, like your wedding?" she suggested. A few more sips of wine and she was almost feeling mellow.

Rachel made a face. "Do you really want to talk about that?"

"Don't you?"

"I suppose, but..." Rachel shrugged. "It seems like the

last thing you need to hear about is bridesmaid dresses and flower arrangements."

With a guilty pang, Esther realized she hadn't really asked Rachel about her wedding plans that much before. She'd given vague glances at bridal magazines and let the talk of dresses and menus during her mother's Sunday dinners wash over her. She'd been too busy with her own worries, her own grief. It seemed selfish now. It *was* selfish.

"How's it all going, anyway?" she asked. "It's only... what, three more months?"

"Three and a half. July fifth."

"So things are coming along, then?"

"I guess." Rachel, normally so bubbly, seemed both unenthused and strangely reluctant to part with any details of the big day.

"Have you picked out a wedding dress? I know you were looking..."

"Not yet. I'm hoping to go down to Manchester in a couple of weeks."

"And bridesmaid dresses, as well?" She, Anna, and Miriam were all going to be bridesmaids. "I hope they're not going to be too naff or revolting."

Rachel let out a gurgle of laughter. "Because that would just be the look I'm going for. Naff *and* revolting."

Esther smiled, enjoying the banter they'd once taken for granted, back when they'd been younger. "You know what I mean."

"I do, because I've looked at more wretched dresses than I can remember, and most of them *have* been both naff and revolting. But I think I've settled on something simple—navy blue, which I don't think you'll mind. I was going to suggest we all go to Manchester for the weekend to try them on, and I'll look at dresses for myself as well, but I didn't want to presume..."

"Presume?"

Rachel shrugged, her gaze sliding away. "You just seem to have a lot going on..."

"Rachel, I'm back to living with our parents. I don't have anything going on."

Rachel brightened. "Then you'll go?"

Would she? She didn't really do girly weekends, and truth be told, neither did her sisters. Rachel was the girliest one of them all, but she tended to do that kind of stuff with her friends rather than flesh and blood.

"I'll go," Esther said, feeling reckless all of a sudden. Maybe it was the wine, or maybe she just really needed a break. A break from herself, if that was even possible. But why not shake things up a little? Even if it involved lurid cocktails and even more lurid dresses.

"Brilliant!" Rachel smiled, looking excited. "How about next weekend?"

"Any weekend but that one," Esther answered with a grimace. "I'm going to Helen's wedding."

"Oh, right. That should be a good 'do." Rachel eyed her

askance. "And Will...?"

"We're going together."

"Oh." Esther watched, bemused, as both surprise and hopeful suspicion flitted across her sister's face. Rachel was remarkably easy to read. "It doesn't mean anything," Esther told her. "We're just keeping up appearances because it's still so early."

"Fine, but why don't you use it as a chance to talk? Properly, I mean? Because, honestly, Esther, I'm not sure you even know why you guys split."

Esther looked away, a suspicious lump forming in her throat. Where had all these wretched hormones come from? "I do know, Rachel, it's just not that easy to put into words."

"Well, it doesn't seem as if Will knows."

"Why? Did he talk to you?" The words came out sharp.

"No, but the man looks as if he'd been poleaxed, Esther. As far as Dan or I can tell, he had no idea this was coming."

"That's because he'd be happy to just keep muddling along," Esther snapped, "and that was part of the problem." But only part, and if she was honest, it wasn't even the biggest part. Still, it was the easiest one to wave like a red flag. Distraction techniques, which was kind of awful.

"Have you told him that?"

"Yes."

Rachel shook her head slowly. "Are you sure this isn't some kind of seven-year itch?"

"I'm not remotely itchy."

"Then what?"

Esther sighed heavily. Why couldn't anyone understand? She knew why, of course; because she wasn't telling anyone the full truth. And she didn't want to. Even so, a little compassionate quiet would not go amiss.

"Sorry," Rachel said. "I'm being pushy, and I said I wouldn't. How about another glass of wine?"

"I can't. I'm driving." Esther heaved herself up from the sofa. "And I should check in with Mum and Dad before they decide to ring the Good Samaritans."

"They mean well."

"They always do, and I don't think I'd want it otherwise, but…" Esther sighed again. "It doesn't always make it easier, does it?"

"No," Rachel agreed. "It doesn't. But it's not an easy situation, is it?"

No, Esther thought as she climbed into her car a few minutes later. It certainly wasn't. And she didn't see it getting easier anytime soon.

Chapter Five

ESTHER STOOD ON the fringe of the crowd of wedding guests clutching a glass of lukewarm champagne that was almost as flat as she was feeling. There was nothing worse than being at a party where everyone was having loads of fun and she couldn't dredge up so much as a smile. Well, she reflected, there was a lot of worse things, actually. This was just the sour cherry on the top of her crappy cake. And ultimately she couldn't blame anyone but herself.

The last week and a half had been about nothing more than going through the motions—work, home, and back again. She'd had dinner with her parents a couple of times, which hadn't been as tense as she'd feared. It never was. Roger had kept up his usual affable conversation, and her mother had made her favourite foods without any fussing, while Esther had been monosyllabic. Honestly, she didn't deserve them. She didn't deserve anyone.

Tears pricked her eyes and Esther blinked them away resolutely. She hadn't cried since the separation, despite the near-constant threat. Now, sitting on the edge of a happy crowd, on her second glass of champagne, the threat felt a little stronger, but one she was still determined to avoid at all costs. Because if she gave into it… well, who knew what would happen then?

She glanced at Will, who was weaving his way through the crowds towards her. He scrubbed up nicely in a navy-blue suit he hadn't worn since her aunt's funeral five years ago, and he kept tugging at his tie. It would have made Esther smile, once. Now it just made her sad, but then everything was making her sad. She was tired of it, and annoyed with herself for being so wretchedly hormonal.

It wasn't as if she was pregnant anymore. In fact, she'd never been pregnant, not really. The baby had never developed; her womb had been empty. A blighted ovum, her GP had said at the follow-up appointment. Usually a woman miscarried earlier than Esther had; apparently her body hadn't got the memo and still kept thinking she was pregnant even when there had been nothing there.

"You want another drink?" Will stood in front of her and nodded towards her now empty glass. She hadn't even realized she'd finished it.

Although she probably shouldn't, Esther shrugged and handed him her empty glass. "Why not? But something else, perhaps. The champagne's gone flat."

"All right." Will turned away, as silent and stoic as he had been this whole trip. The two-hour drive to Newcastle had been conducted in rather grim silence, with Will staring straight ahead as Esther looked blindly at the barren hills rolling into the distance, dotted with a few sheep, some gambolling lambs. Neither of them had said a single word.

A few months or years ago, the silence wouldn't have bothered her. She would have stretched her feet out on the dash and made a few idle comments. Will would have smiled, that quirk of his lips she'd found so sexy, right from the first moment she'd met him. She wouldn't have questioned *anything,* and part of her still longed for that blissful ignorance, before she'd been awakened to the lack in their relationship, and more crucially, the terrible lack in herself.

"Here you go." Will handed her a drink and after the first sip Esther realized it was a Tom Collins, her favourite cocktail. She hadn't had one in ages, and she probably didn't need the extra alcohol now, but she knocked half of it back in one go. "Thanks."

Will was nursing the same pint of bitter he'd had all evening. He never drank anything else. He stood next to her, as he had for most of the reception, and stared straight ahead. They wouldn't dance, of course. They wouldn't even think of dancing. And normally that would be okay, she wouldn't mind. She wouldn't want to dance, and she didn't really want to now, and yet… something was missing.

"Do you want to dance?"

"What?" Esther turned to him in shock, nearly spitting out a mouthful of gin and lemon. She almost thought she'd fantasized him asking. Will was so not a dancer. They hadn't

even danced at their wedding.

"Do you want to dance?" He didn't sound particularly enthused by the idea, and his jaw was locked tight as he nodded towards the dance floor. "Beats standing here like a pair of lemons, don't you think?"

Esther glanced from him towards the dance floor, heaving with people who were demonstrating their finesse, or lack of it, with the whip and nae nae. She'd already watched several giggly grandmothers doing an exuberant Macarena, wiggling their jiggly hips with enthusiasm.

"I…" She hesitated, wondering at her own reluctance. She'd just been bemoaning having to stand here watching everyone else have fun, and now Will was giving her another option. "I suppose," she said, and finished her drink before putting the glass aside. "Why not?"

They'd just stepped onto the dance floor when the music changed from the pumped-up techno of "Watch Me" to the heartrending and rather sappy strains of "The Wind Beneath My Wings."

Will looked, for a second, as if he wanted to bolt from the floor. Couples were coming together all around them like it was a Year Seven disco, arms locked around waists, hands on shoulders, hips swaying as Bette Midler belted it out.

Did you ever know that you're my hero…

Now, instead of safely on the side, they were standing in the middle of the dance floor like lemons.

"Well?" Will held his arms out and Esther stepped closer

to him, placing her hands lightly on his strong shoulders as his arms came around her waist and like everyone else they started to sway.

This wasn't so bad. Neither of them were dancers, heaven knew, but in some ways this was easier than attempting to dab or something equally ridiculous.

Then Will pulled her a little closer, so their hips nudged, and despite everything, or perhaps because of it, heat and longing both flared inside her. Instinctively her hands tightened on his shoulders, and Will noticed, his eyes narrowing as he gazed down at her. Esther dropped her gaze and focused on their shuffling feet.

She felt the longing well up inside her, but for what she couldn't say. Impossible things, she supposed. For Will to be different, for her to be different, for life to be different. Yet nothing was—except maybe she was, because she felt so flattened, so unable. Usually, she picked herself up and kept moving, but now she felt as if she was standing in the middle of a road, waiting to be mown down. She was exasperated with herself, and yet she still couldn't seem to move.

They swayed silently, bodies brushing, the room feeling as if it were fading in and out. Esther breathed in the smell of Will—old-fashioned aftershave and a hint of lanolin, from being with sheep all day. As she dared to raise her head again, she saw he'd nicked his jaw when he'd shaved that morning, and he'd also missed a bit by his ear. Awkwardly, she caught his gaze, saw the heat in his eyes, and felt jolted. Was he noticing the same kinds of details about her? Was he looking at her the way she was at him, remembering when things had seemed simple, had felt easy? Could it ever feel that way again?

The song felt as if it were going on forever, and Esther didn't know whether she wanted it to end or not.

Eventually the song did end, replaced by an eye-wateringly loud pop song, something neither of them recognized. They stepped apart almost guiltily, or perhaps that was just her.

"Do you want another drink?" Will asked.

"I really shouldn't." She was already fairly sozzled, and she felt now that she needed her wits about her. Everything was starting to feel heartrendingly complicated, the longing and the loneliness, the guilt and the grief.

"Suit yourself."

And now there they were, standing on the side, a pair of lemons. "Maybe we should just go," Esther blurted, and Will cocked an eyebrow.

"Helen and Nate haven't left yet."

"I know, but…" Esther shrugged. Helen was still high-kicking her heels on the dance floor, and Esther suspected the reception would last into the wee hours. "We've been here for a while."

"True." She couldn't tell anything from Will's tone. "Fine." He jerked one powerful shoulder. "Let's go."

"We should make our excuses to Helen first." Belatedly

Esther realized that hadn't been the best choice of words. They wended their way through the gyrating crowd, bumping awkwardly with overenthusiastic dancers, before Esther managed to tap her friend on the shoulder.

"Helen…"

"Oy!" Helen grabbed both of her hands and spun her around before Esther could stammer her goodbye. The room spun, as did the alcohol in her stomach. In the blur around her she saw Will, standing still and stony, reminding her of one of those monoliths on Easter Island. Completely intractable and fairly out of place.

"Come dance," Helen called to him, and then she was grabbing his hand, clearly three sheets to the wind, or perhaps even half a dozen. Will toppled more than moved, nearly losing his balance as Helen yanked on his arm and then somehow they were all dancing to that inane but catchy song "Call Me Maybe," and Esther, for some odd reason, was belting out the lyrics along with everyone else, even though she hadn't realized she'd known them, and she certainly wasn't the sort of person to sing along to, well, anything. She really was drunk.

Will wasn't dancing so much as shifting from foot to foot, but at least he was trying, although why that mattered Esther couldn't even say. Then he caught her eye and gave her the tiniest quirk of a smile, and her stomach turned right over. She felt young again; she remembered, and she *felt*.

Then the song ended, and Will stepped quickly off the

dance floor. Helen went to get a drink, and dutifully Esther followed her, that brief moment of solidarity and sentiment vanished in the flick of an eyelid, the switch of a song.

"So, how are you two?" Helen asked as she guzzled a glass of champagne—from a fresh bottle, judging from the fizziness. "I feel as if we haven't talked properly in ages."

"I know." This didn't seem like the best time to say she was leaving the party, or that she and Will were separated, or… anything. "It's been a fantastic do, Helen, but…"

"Oh, and it's just beginning!" Helen's eyes narrowed. "You two aren't going to go all damp squibby on me, are you?"

"Well, the thing is, Will's tired from lambing season…"

Helen rolled her eyes. "Excuses! But, seriously…" She glanced at Esther, and then at Will, who was standing behind her and hadn't said a word. "Is everything okay?"

How to answer that? Esther stared at her friend for a moment, her chest going tight, Will waiting for her reply. She couldn't possibly go into it now. "Yeah, yeah," she finally said, summoning a smile. "We're fine. 'Course we are. What about you? How's Natural England on this side of the Pennines?"

"Didn't I tell you? I'm taking the redundancy package."

"You are?" Esther blinked in surprise. She'd always thought Helen was as wed to her job as Esther was. They'd started as raw recruits together, twenty-two years old and blazing self-righteous determination to change the world, or at least the farmland of England's northwest. "Why?"

Helen rolled her eyes. "Rumour has it that plenty of people are going to get the chop soon, especially if you work full-time. Too expensive."

"Yes, but…" Esther stared at her helplessly. Natural England was always cutting costs, corners, and yes, staff, but Esther had somehow thought she and Helen were immune. They were both lifers, committed to the cause. Everyone knew that. She'd never wavered in her devotion to her job, crappy as it could sometimes be. Never, ever. It had been one thing anchoring her when everything else had started to waver.

Helen must have seen something of the surprise and distress in her face because she softened, placing one hand on Esther's shoulder. "It's not the same as it was, is it?" she said in the tone of someone talking to someone recently bereaved. "Not like when we started, and we were doing five or six farm visits a week, feeling like we were really accomplishing something. Do you remember?" Helen let out a sigh of pure nostalgia. "Coaxing some old codger into signing up for the environmental scheme, and seeing how pleased he was when it actually worked? When was the last time that happened?"

"Well…"

"Now there are so many blasted hoops for the farmers to jump through and we're the ones holding them out, higher and higher. They never can do enough to get into the schemes, and it takes years to get one signed on properly, never mind the numbers we really need to make a difference." Helen shook her head. "I still love the ethos, and I always will, but I can't stand the bureaucracy. I've spent more time filling out spreadsheets about how I'm performing on the job than *doing* my job. I'm getting out while I can. They won't be offering these redundancy packages forever, you know. A year or two from now it'll be a shove in the back and a 'thanks very much.' A knees-up in the staff room if you're lucky with a bottle of plonk, and that's it." Helen looked positively grim for a few seconds, as Esther struggled to absorb all she'd said.

"Perhaps, but… what will you do instead?" Esther couldn't imagine doing anything else. She wasn't trained for anything else. She had a degree in land management and ten years of experience with one government agency. Suddenly it seemed like very little.

"Who knows?" Helen shrugged. "Take a break, start a farm shop, go freelance?" She gave one of her old cheeky grins. "First I'm going to enjoy my honeymoon!"

They chatted for a few more minutes, mostly about Helen and Nate's honeymoon to Ibiza, and then, after a couple of hugs and smoochy kisses on both cheeks, she and Will were free. Esther stepped out into the night, breathing in the cool, smog-scented air.

The empty street seemed quiet after the crashing pop music of the party, the ensuing silence taut.

"Sorry about all that," Esther said, and Will shrugged.

"I don't mind a bit of a boogey," he said with the faintest glimmer of a smile.

A surprised bubble of laughter escaped her. "I thought you hated dancing."

"Hate is a strong word."

Everything seemed loaded with subtext, but Esther didn't know if she was simply imagining that. Will wasn't exactly a subtext sort of man, was he? He was as straight and upfront as they came. What she saw was what she got. Which could be either a good or bad thing.

"Let's find the hotel," she said, and scrolled on her phone for directions sent in the confirmation email. They hadn't had a chance to check-in before going to the wedding, and Esther supposed it was just as well. It was going to be awkward enough sharing a room and most likely a bed without having had to have been reminded of it beforehand.

They got their overnight bags from Will's car in the nearby car park, and then made the ten-minute walk to the hotel along the narrow, darkened streets of Newcastle's downtown, the only sounds the blare of a distant car horn, and the faint shouts of someone being ejected from a pub, one street over. Neither of them spoke.

They arrived at the hotel, a narrow building crammed between large, modern monstrosities, and after a few minutes to check-in, they were upstairs in a room that was, Esther saw with a sinking sensation, really quite tiny. A double bed, not the queen she'd been hoping for, and about a foot between it and the bureau. The adjoining bathroom was small enough to make using the loo and the shower at the same time possible, if she'd wished to attempt such a feat of hydraulic engineering.

"Well, this is cosy." Will hefted both their bags onto the bureau. With the two of them in it the room felt even tinier, airless. Her head was still spinning from all the alcohol she'd ill-advisedly imbibed.

"I think I'll take a shower."

"Fine by me."

Unfortunately, Esther realized after she'd shimmied past Will to collect her washbag, the bathroom had a door constructed entirely of frosted glass, and made her feel as if she were performing in a peep show. It was impossible not to have her full silhouette be visible, and also impossible, considering the size of the room, not to have Will watch—all which made having a shower a far less relaxing proposition than she'd hoped.

It felt stupid to be self-conscious considering how well Will knew her body, and how she knew his. Every scar, every sinew, everything. They'd been married for seven years. Of course they knew each other, physically at least.

Yet now, as she rinsed off as quickly as she should, and then yanked on her sensible pyjamas—a fleece top and yoga pants—she felt ridiculously prudish, as if she'd turned into a buttoned-up nun. She avoided looking at Will as she hurried into bed.

He was already lying on one side of what now seemed like the tiniest double bed ever known to humankind, staring up at the ceiling, his hands folded over his broad—and bare—chest like a corpse in a casket.

As Esther slid into her side of the bed, she thought about asking him to put on a shirt, and then decided not to go there. She turned so her back was to Will and clicked off the light.

Silence smothered the room, heavy and oppressive. Esther scrunched her eyes shut, as if she could forcibly will herself to sleep. She edged her feet away from Will's, in case they tangled toes as they so often had in the past, their version of a kiss good-night.

"Nice door on the bathroom," Will commented after several endless minutes, his voice disembodied in the darkness, and Esther's whole body jolted with tension, as well as something else.

"You didn't have to look."

"Kind of hard not to, and in any case, we're married." Will shifted on the bed so his body, already mere inches from hers, pressed that much closer. "I know your body as well as my own, Esther." He spoke matter-of-factly but it still made a shiver go through her. She'd been thinking the same thing, and to hear Will say it made heat bloom inside her.

Then Will put his hand on her shoulder, heavy and warm. "Esther..."

Esther didn't know who moved first. Did she roll over, or did Will pull her toward him? Somehow they were face to face, hip to hip, toes tangling as they always did. And then Will was kissing her, big, greedy, swallowing kisses that made her feel both desired and obliterated. They'd been apart for two measly weeks but it felt like a lifetime, a very lonely lifetime, and Will's arms were strong, his body solid, everything about him familiar in a way that didn't feel aggravating or depressing, just good.

Sex would complicate things, but then again, maybe it wouldn't. After all, they were married, and it was something they'd done a thousand times before. A bodily function, a basic urge... the way to make a baby.

It was the last that caught her like a fist to the gust, a karate chop to her heart. She stilled underneath Will—at some point he'd rolled on top of her, one large, callused palm sliding underneath her fleece top and fighting a deep-seated urge both to give in and to scream, Esther pushed his hand away.

"No. I'm sorry, but no."

He stilled on top of her, one hand resting on the flat of her stomach. "Esther..."

"I—" She drew a quick breath. Her mind was blank, her body pulsing, no longer with desire, but with pain.

Will rolled off her. "Esther," he said again, and it was half-statement, half-question.

Esther stared up at the ceiling, the only sound Will's

steady breathing, as well as the ragged hitch of her own. She was not going to cry. She was not. If she cried now, she'd be done for. She'd plunge into those dark depths and never resurface.

"I'm sorry," she managed to choke out. "I... I just can't."

Chapter Six

DISAPPOINTMENT AND WORSE, hurt, flooded through Will. All right, maybe sex hadn't been the best idea right now, but he hadn't had any others and having Esther in his arms had been the best thing that had happened to him in ages. He'd felt as if something inside him that had been off-balance for the last few weeks had finally, thankfully, been righted, only to now have it sent spinning again.

Esther drew a quick, raggedy sort of breath, and Will sat up and switched on the light. In the murky, low-watt glow of the bedside table lamp, he saw her staring resolutely at the ceiling, her jaw clenched tight, her expression stony, as if she was enduring what had just happened between them. As if she hadn't been kissing him back with as much urgency and excitement as he had. Anger flared low in his belly, like a warning shot. He took a steadying breath, determined not to give into that flare of temper.

"What's going on, Esther?"

She bit her lip. "What do you mean?"

"What do I *mean?* You look like you've been having to

grin and bear it, but that wasn't what was going on here, least not as far as I could tell, and I *could* tell." He didn't think he was that off the mark, surely.

"I… I don't want to complicate things." Her voice was wooden.

"Then you shouldn't have bloody left!" The words were practically a roar, bursting out of him, surprising them both. Will fell back against the pillows and closed his eyes, trying to hold onto his calm. "Something's not making sense, Esther, because I don't think I'm that stupid. You haven't told me you don't love me, and a few moments ago you were showing me that you did, least how I see it."

"Don't, Will—"

"Don't what?" He opened his eyes and stared at her. "Don't make love to my wife? Don't say the truth? Except I don't think I even know what the truth is, and you're sure not saying it." Although the truth was, he didn't even know if there was something she wasn't saying, and that both annoyed and scared him. A part of him couldn't help but think Esther was making a fuss over nothing—but right now it felt like a lot of nothing.

"I don't know if I can explain," she said at last, her gaze still fixed on the ceiling.

"Try." He gazed at her steadily while she stayed flat on her back and stared straight up. "I think I deserve that much. What's going on?" Although why he expected truth now, he didn't even know, because he hadn't had a straight answer from his wife since this whole mess had begun.

"I'm not sure I could even tell you." Her words were indistinct through her barely moving lips, her hands clenched by her sides.

"If you try, maybe I'll understand."

Esther shook her head, taking a deep breath as she finally looked at him, her face full of misery. "Oh, Will, I don't think you would."

Something in her tone made a shiver of dread, ice-cold and awful, go through him. "Why wouldn't I?"

"I'm afraid you'd… you'd think of me differently. Badly. And despite everything, I'd hate that."

The dread was creeping through him like a cold mist, snaking its tendrils around his heart, turning everything to ice. "Why?" Esther just shook her head again, and Will forced himself to say the words that were forming in his head through numb lips. "Esther, have you been… have you been having an affair?"

"An *affair?*" The two words were a screech of incredulous indignation that, impossibly, made Will smile. He knew right then what the answer was, and he was glad, although he was sorry he'd actually had to ask the question, especially when Esther scrambled off the bed, straightening her fleece top with shaking hands. "How can you ask me that?"

"Because you left me," Will returned, his voice harder than he'd meant it to be. Anger flared through him again, even though he'd been trying to suppress it. "And you didn't give me a reason, and I'd thought we were fine."

"Exactly—"

"Be straight with me, Esther. What have I been meant to think?"

"Not that." Her lips trembled and she pressed them together. "For heaven's sake, not that."

"Then what?" Will demanded. "Because nothing you've said has made any sense to me."

She didn't answer, and he stared at her in a mixture of exasperation and defeat. "You're still not going to tell me, are you? Whatever it is." Although he supposed he should be glad that it was at least something. The last time they'd talked Esther had been so dispiritedly vague he had wondered if there really was any reason she'd left him. Maybe she'd just stopped loving him, like a car that had run out of petrol. Nothing more to give.

"I didn't want our baby," she said in a low voice, not looking at him. Will struggled to hear the words, and then to make sense of them. *Didn't want?* Esther wasn't looking at him, her face averted, her expression completely closed.

"You—what?" He stared at her in confusion.

"I didn't want our baby," she repeated more distinctly. "I didn't want to get pregnant. I never wanted to have a family."

He stared at her, completely at a loss. "Why didn't you say something, then?" he finally asked. "When we started trying?"

"I don't know." Esther's voice was soft and sad, so unlike her normal voice. She was always so brisk, so decisive about everything. Will tried to remember back to when they'd decided to try for a baby. They hadn't had much of a conversation about it, as far as he could recall, but it had seemed natural. Normal. Had he brought it up first? He must have, but he couldn't remember now.

"I don't understand you," he said after a moment, because he didn't and he had no other words.

"I know." She sat on the edge of the bed, her dark hair swinging down to brush her cheek, her expression hidden. "I'm sorry."

"For what, exactly?"

"Being confusing, I suppose. And for... for not being who you thought I was. What you want."

"How do you know you're not what I want?" His head felt fuzzy, too full with thoughts and feelings, this new information that he didn't know what to do with.

"I mean... a mother..." She trailed off miserably.

"But..." He shook his head slowly. "If you'd told me beforehand..." He couldn't finish that thought. If she'd told him she didn't want kids, how would he have felt? He didn't even know. He'd just assumed they wanted the same things, because they always had. And why wouldn't she want a child? Wasn't that the way of things, especially in their part of the world? They married, they had kids, they got old together. Had he presumed too much, to think that was how it would go with them? She'd never said differently.

"If I'd told you that I didn't want your child?" Esther looked up, a look of surprise and something almost like scorn on her face, making Will recoil. He hadn't thought of it quite like that. "That I don't ever want that? And," she added, her voice shaking, "that when I saw that blank ultrasound screen and realized there was no baby, you know the first thing I felt? Do you want to know? Do you want me to tell you, Will?"

"Esther..." It came out as a warning. He didn't want to hear. He knew he didn't.

"Relief," she said flatly, her face turned away from him. "I felt relieved, Will, that there was no baby. Relieved that I could walk away from it without it being my fault, pack up the baby clothes and the prenatal vitamins, all of it. All the things I never wanted. I didn't have to do any of it, and I was relieved." Her voice shook and she wrapped her arms around herself, a picture of a woman in grief, and yet she wasn't.

Will shook his head, unable to process it all, or at least not wanting to. *I didn't want your child. I don't ever want your child.* And she'd been relieved by their miscarriage, actually *glad*. Was she trying to make him hate her? Or did she just hate him that much?

His head swam and he felt sick. It was so much worse than he'd thought. He almost wished Esther had had an affair. That would have been easier to understand, to accept, than the cold disdain she was subjecting him to now, the near sneer he'd heard in her voice. Why had she married him in the first place? Had she ever loved him?

"I…" He rose for the bed, yanking a T-shirt over his head. "I need some air."

Her eyes widened. "Where are you going?"

"Out." He couldn't think in this tiny room that felt airless, claustrophobic with memories and words that could not be unspoken. He'd never not know these things now.

"Fine." Esther curled up on the bed, her eyes dark and wide as Will jammed his feet into his dress shoes, the only pair he'd brought, stupidly. He grabbed his coat and wrenched the door open, needing only to get away. Esther didn't say anything as he went; she didn't even look in his direction as he left, the door slamming shut behind him.

ESTHER LAY BACK on the bed, her knees tucked up to her chest, everything in her aching although her eyes were thankfully dry and her head felt clear. At least now he knew. Perhaps she hadn't needed to say it so starkly, but it was the truth, and that was something she'd kept from Will too long. Telling him had felt a bit like lancing a wound, relieving that dreadful pressure, but once the immediate relief eased up, which it already had, she was left with the blaze of pain of an open injury that still needed to heal. Maybe it never would.

Even though she was glad Will knew, that she didn't

have to hide it anymore, she hated the thought of him looking at her differently. Maybe he'd hate her. Was that why he'd had to leave? Because he couldn't bear to be in the same room with her, the abnormal woman who hadn't wanted her husband's baby, who had been relieved by what should have been a tragedy? She hated herself; it made sense for Will to hate her too. She almost wanted him to hate her, and maybe that was why she'd said what she had, *his* baby, making it as personal and cruel as possible, because having Will hate her felt right, the punishment she deserved. How crazy and messed up *was* she?

Eventually she fell into an uneasy doze, only to wake in the middle of the night; someone was shouting in the street below, but she couldn't make out the words. Esther fumbled for her phone and saw that it was nearly four in the morning, and Will hadn't come back.

Her stomach felt hollowed out and she knew she wouldn't get back to sleep. She dressed and made herself a cup of awful instant coffee with the little kettle perched on the top of the bureau, and then sat on the edge of the bed drinking it until a greyish morning light filtered through the curtains.

Her mind was blank and she didn't know how many minutes or hours had passed until she heard the key turning in the lock and then Will was there, looking exhausted and unshaven.

"Where did you sleep?" Esther asked, and he shrugged.

"In the car."

There didn't seem to be anything more to say than that. She had no idea how to bridge this chasm that had opened between them, a chasm absolutely of her own making. They packed up in silence and were headed back to Thornthwaite before it had gone six.

"Esther." Ruth Holley's expression was almost comical as Esther came into the kitchen of the vicarage two and a half hours later, feeling completely grotty. Will hadn't said a word as he'd pulled into the farmyard. Not one word as he'd got out and then gone right to the lambing shed. Esther had watched him go, wondering what on earth she wanted him to say. What could she even expect him to say? Then she'd climbed into her car and driven to the vicarage, because where else was she going to go?

Ruth gazed at her in open concern as she dumped her bag on the kitchen table, among the breakfast dishes. Her mother was dressed for church because it was, of course, Sunday, and she whisked away several dirty plates so Esther could sit down at a clean space. "I didn't expect you back so early… is everything all right?"

"There wasn't any real reason to stay."

"Have you eaten…"

"I'm not hungry, but I could murder a cup of tea."

"Of course." Her mother had already switched on the kettle as a matter of habit. She frowned at Esther as she got out a mug and teabag. Esther dropped her head into her hands, because she felt so very tired, and even worse, defeated. Like nothing mattered anymore, because maybe it didn't.

"Esther…"

"Not now, Mum." Esther forced herself to lift her head and meet her mother's worried gaze. "I can't talk about it now."

"I know you can't," Ruth answered, her tone managing to hold both asperity and gentleness. "I wasn't going to ask you anything. But maybe you should do something else. Get out of yourself for a bit." She paused. "You could come to church."

Esther tried not to cringe. Coming along to the morning service would delight both her parents, but she couldn't summon the energy, never mind the desire.

"Sorry, but I'm just too shattered." The kettle bubbled and then switched off, seeming to plunge the room into silence. "I think I'll just go to bed."

Ruth nodded. "All right, darling," she said, clearly trying not to sound disappointed. "I'm sure you could do with a good kip." She made Esther a mug of tea and Esther sat and sipped it, feeling wretched, while her mother moved around her, cleaning up.

"Leave it," she said after a few minutes, half because she felt guilty simply sitting there, and half because she wanted to be alone. "I'll tidy up while you're at church."

"All right…"

"Is anyone coming for Sunday lunch?" Someone usually

was.

"Not this Sunday."

"I'll make us all something, then," Esther said, although she couldn't imagine finding the energy or the will.

"Get some sleep first," her mother advised. She still looked terribly worried.

After Ruth had gone, Esther dragged herself upstairs for a shower before she fell into bed, curling into a ball, knees tucked to her chest. In the distance she heard the peal of church bells and the sound of her father's modest flock coming into church. It was a cheerful sound, the soundtrack of her childhood, but right now it just made her sad. Everything did. When she closed her eyes, she saw the look of shock and then something far too close to revulsion on Will's face.

I don't want to have your child. Why had she said it like that, as if she was disgusted by him? Had she been trying to hurt him, or had she simply wanted him to see the ugliness inside her that she'd been trying to hide for so long?

It didn't really matter though. The outcome was the same. Will wouldn't contest the separation, or even the divorce. Not now that he knew the truth.

She woke eventually, blinking muzzily in the gloom of her little bedroom under the eaves; she could hear the patter of rain against the roof and it was a strangely comforting sound. A glance at the clock made her realize she'd missed lunch, never mind making something for her parents. Esther yanked on a fleece as well as ran a brush through her unruly hair, and then headed downstairs.

The vicarage was quiet, so different from the chaotic bustle of her childhood, or the times when she usually came here, which was for family dinners and holiday celebrations. Esther saw that her father's study door was closed, which meant he wasn't to be disturbed, and so she made her way back to the kitchen, only to find it empty, a note on the table from her mother saying she'd left a plate in the oven for her.

Esther took out the pasta bake that had dried out, developing a hardened crust, but she ate it anyway, more out of guilt than anything else. Then she went to find her mother, only to find room after room empty and silent. The house felt eerily emptily, despite the fact she knew her father had to be closeted in his study, no doubt preparing for his evening sermon.

The family TV room upstairs was empty as well, as was her parents' bedroom. Unsure even now why she was looking so persistently; her mother might be out, after all, Esther peeked in the empty bedrooms upstairs only to come to a shocked stand still when she found her mother in her brother Jamie's old room, sitting on the edge of the bed, a distant look on her face as she gazed out the window at the stark and leafless cherry tree in the vicarage's Victorian walled garden.

"Mum…" Esther half-wished she hadn't said anything; her mother looked as if she were having a private moment. Yet she had, and Ruth turned to her, startled out of her moment of contemplation.

"Hello, darling. Are you feeling better?"

"What are you doing in here?"

Ruth shrugged, smoothing one palm over the duvet. "I like to come in here sometimes."

Esther took a step into the room. She hadn't been in here since before Jamie had died, she realized with a jolt. Had she been avoiding the room subconsciously?

"Why do you come in here?" she asked quietly.

Ruth's lowered gaze remained on the duvet. "I know it doesn't really make a difference, but I feel closer to Jamie in here. I feel as if there are more memories here than by some cold headstone in the churchyard."

"Do you miss him?" Esther asked, realizing at once it was a completely idiotic question. It might have been twenty years, but Esther knew you never stopped missing someone you loved. Never.

"Every day." Ruth's mouth curved in a small, sad smile. "Every single day."

"Oh, Mum." Esther sank onto the bed next to her mother and, somewhat awkwardly, put her arm around Ruth's shoulders. She'd never been much of one for physical affection, whether with family or regarding romance; sex or smiles, that was pretty much it in her repertoire. But now, feeling so jagged and broken inside, and suspecting her mother, her calm, capable, always smiling mum, might feel a little bit of the same way, compelled her to offer what little she could. "I'm sorry."

"So am I." Ruth squeezed her arm, briefly leaning her head against her shoulder. "So am I, darling. But one thing I've learned in this world is that grief and suffering are always going to happen. You might be able to avoid them for a while, but they'll still come for you eventually. It's how you respond to it that matters."

Uh-oh. Esther straightened, giving her mum an uncertain smile. Here came the lecture. "Is this where you tell me to keep my chin up and pull myself up by my emotional bootstraps?"

"Emotional bootstraps?" Ruth looked bemused. "Heavens, no. That sounds awful. No, Esther, this is where I tell you that I can see how unhappy you are, and how hurt, and I know that sometimes there is no way but through it, just as if you're going on a bear hunt." Esther laughed softly at the mention of the children's story.

"We can't go under it, we can't go over it…" She quoted with a sigh. If only.

"But you don't have to go through it alone," Ruth continued quietly. "And you don't have to drag your feet and hang your head the whole time. Let us help you, my darling. Let us in."

"Oh, Mum." There were the tears, always lurking, threatening to spill from her eyes, the sobs from her mouth. She swallowed hard. "I don't think you really want you know."

"Do you think," Ruth asked seriously, "that anything you say could change the way your father or I feel about you? Anything at all?"

Esther swallowed the lump in her throat down, determined to remain dry-eyed. "I don't know," she admitted, and her mother's face crumpled a little bit. "That's a reflection of me, not you," she hastened to add.

Ruth sighed and rose from the bed. "It's a reflection of both of us. But I hope you'll be able to share whatever it is that is tormenting you, Esther, because I promise you, your father and I love you very much, more than you could ever know, and we just want to help."

"I know," Esther whispered, feeling more wretched than ever. "Thank you."

Her mother smiled and patted her cheek. "If ever you feel like talking, you know we're here," she said sadly, and left the room.

Chapter Seven

THE VICARAGE WAS quiet as Esther set up work in the kitchen, the warmest room, the next morning, Charlie stretched out by her feet and the Aga emitting a comforting warmth. Her father was working in the study and Ruth had gone out grocery shopping. For a few minutes, as Esther sipped her second cup of tea, she let herself appreciate the peace and solitude.

She had no farm visits to make, just eight hours of emails and spreadsheets awaiting her, but mind-numbing work could be a good thing. After Ruth's honest conversation with Esther in Jamie's old bedroom, her feelings were in a ferment. She'd come surprisingly close to spilling everything to her mum, had thought about it for a few heart-stopping seconds, but some thread of self-preservation had held her back. Will already looked at her differently. She couldn't stand it if her parents did, as well.

And yet something had to change. The frank talk with her mum had made Esther realize that. She couldn't go on like this, miserable and hurting, life feeling like a swamp she had to struggle through. Something had to change, only she didn't know what. With a sigh and a sip of tea, she clicked on her inbox, only to frown at the email from the head office. Those were usually ominous.

And this one was, in a way—the head office was offering another round of redundancy packages to anyone who was willing to quit. Usually Esther would just delete it without a thought, and yet now, thinking of Helen, she paused. *They won't offer redundancy packages forever.* No, at some point they'd just lay people off with nothing, maybe not even the knees-up Helen had scoffingly referenced.

It seemed they were always needing to reduce numbers, something Esther had always found frustrating because while the work increased, the people doing it always diminished, making a job she'd once loved turn into something impossible to do.

But now, sipping her tea, thinking of Helen, she started to wonder. Dream a little, which was something she hadn't done in ages, if ever. Think outside this depressingly small box. So what if she took one of those redundancy packages? She needed a change; what if this was it?

And Helen had been right when she'd said their jobs weren't what they once had been, back when they'd both been fresh-faced and optimistic.

Now the environmental schemes had a thousand hoops to jump through, and farmers were more and more reluctant to sign up. The amount of red tape to do anything meant that eighty percent of Esther's job wasn't out on a farm or field, but sitting in front of her laptop, squinting at a spreadsheet.

So what if she quit? It felt both liberating and terrifying even to think of it. To wonder. She didn't have Will or the farm to think about anymore, as much as that pained her. For once in her life she was a free agent. She could do what she liked.

Of course, if she quit Natural England, she had no idea what she'd do. What she was qualified for, or what she even wanted. She'd never done anything else, ever. And it seemed to take away something that had defined her, when she already felt as if she were spinning in a void.

"Esther?" Ruth called as the front door opened, letting in a gust of cold wind that made it all the way to the kitchen. Charlie lifted his head briefly, sniffed the air, and then dropped his muzzle back onto his paws with a sigh.

"Do you need help?" Esther closed her laptop and rose from the table, leaving the warmth of the kitchen for the icy draughtiness of the front hall.

Fifteen minutes later she'd helped Ruth load all the bags into the kitchen, and was now putting away packets and tins in the walk-in pantry, one of two that the vicarage had.

"How are things?" Ruth asked as she folded up the bags and stuffed them in the cupboard under the kitchen sink. "Cracking on with work?"

"Not really." Esther leaned against the door to the pantry, her arms folded. "Actually, I received a message from the head office offering decent redundancy packages to those who want to quit." She paused as Ruth looked at her, eyebrows raised expectantly. "I thought I might take one." Just saying the words sent a thrill through her, although of excitement or terror she didn't know. Probably both.

"Really?" Ruth frowned. "But I thought you liked your job."

"I did, but it's changed so much over the years and now I spend most of my time doing data entry and answering emails." Esther shrugged. "Plus I could do with a change." Maybe she was mad even to think about it.

"So what would you do instead?"

"I have no idea." Esther sat back down at the table with a sigh. It *was* a mad idea. Of course it was. "I don't know why I thought of it, really."

"Life feels unsettled," Ruth said, placing one hand on Esther's shoulder. "I understand the desire and even the need to make some kind of change. I just want you to be sure this is the right one."

"Well, if you think getting back with Will is the right one, you're wrong," Esther said, knowing she sounded querulous and childish, but unable to keep herself from it. She knew what her mother was thinking. Wanting. "Not that he even wants to get back together with me anymore."

Ruth's frown deepened. "What do you mean?"

"Just that." A wretched lump was forming in her throat

again. "He's woken up to the truth, just as I have."

"Esther…"

"I should work," Esther said, and opened her laptop. She didn't want to talk about Will. She couldn't. Ruth left her in peace a few minutes later, but Esther didn't feel peaceful. She felt unsettled and unhappy and restless, and after a couple of hours of ploughing through spreadsheets she got up and whistled for Charlie, who lifted his greying head and blinked at her in sleepy shock.

"Come on," she said as she reached for his lead. "You still like your walkies, don't you, old boy?"

Charlie lumbered to his feet and Esther pulled on her coat and a pair of Wellies from the porch. A few minutes later she was heading down the church lane, the day brisk and chilly, with weak, watery sunlight filtering through the clouds and illuminating the fells in all their frost-covered glory. Spring was on the horizon, but it felt like no more than a breath in the air on a frosty day like today.

She walked quickly, her head down and chin tucked low, the way she always walked, Charlie doing his best to keep up with her. She was so intent on striding along that she didn't realize she'd nearly careened into someone until his hands were on her arms and he was steadying her. Esther came to an abrupt and shocked halt, blinking up at the friendly face of a man she vaguely recognized.

"Whoa, there, you're in a hurry." His smile was wide and easy. "Esther, isn't it?"

"Yes…" Was it someone from church? She couldn't place him, with his dark hair and dimples, about the same age as she was. She didn't think they'd gone to school or youth group together, either. "Sorry…"

"Mark," he smiled. "Mark Taylor. I teach at the primary, with your sister Rachel. I do music lessons."

"Oh, right…"

"We met at a Christmas party she dragged you to, years ago. I doubt you remember."

She didn't, and Mark laughed, unbothered. "Anyway, it seems as if you were going somewhere in a hurry, and I'm late for my Year Fours."

"Okay." She stepped aside, watching him go up the steep little lane to the primary school. She had no recollection of meeting him, although she did remember the Christmas party. It had been at The Queen's Sorrow and she'd gone with Rachel because her sister had recently broken up with a boyfriend—there had been several over the years—and she wanted a plus one. Esther had filled in and Will had stayed at home.

With a sigh, Esther kept walking. Her mind felt as if it were flying in a dozen different directions, wondering what her future could hold. If she took the redundancy package, she could move. Travel. Do anything she wanted. Why did that thought of leaving Thornthwaite make her feel anxious and more ambivalent, more immobilized, than ever?

She walked all the way to the top of Thornthwaite, by

the new estate of smart brick houses that the old guard of the village had protested a dozen years ago, which, she supposed, didn't make them that new anymore, never mind she remembered them being built.

Charlie was starting to look tired, his tongue lolling out, his expression hopeful, and Esther knelt to caress his ears.

"Sorry, old boy, I can see you're tired. We'll head back now."

Back at the vicarage her father was in his study with the door open, the woodstove crackling with a merry blaze. He beckoned her in as soon as Esther had shed her coat and Wellies, Charlie retreating gratefully to his place by the Aga.

"Esther, come in. Sit with me a minute."

All through her childhood, invitations into her father's inner sanctum had been relatively rare. Esther could remember going into the study only if she'd been in trouble or in need of a serious talking-to about some area of her life—A levels, university plans, her proposed summer holiday to Corfu when she was nineteen.

It was a testament to her current life situation that she didn't know which one it was now—was she in trouble? Or did she simply need sorting out?

She stepped into her father's study slowly, taking in the faded Oriental carpet, the heavy velvet drapes that were now pulled across the high sashed windows, the towering bookshelves of well-thumbed theology books and the two ancient armchairs by the wood stove. She didn't think the room had changed in thirty years.

"What is it, Dad?"

"Sit down." Roger beckoned to the armchair opposite him. "Stay awhile."

"All right." She perched on the armchair, holding her hands out to the wood stove's cheery warmth. She hadn't realized how cold she'd become on her walk.

"Your mother tells me you're thinking of taking redundancy." So a talking-to about life decisions it was.

"Thinking of it," she agreed. "I only got the email this morning." She brought her hands away from the stove, lacing them together in her lap. She felt as if she were about sixteen. "I suppose you don't think that's a good idea."

Roger smiled in his easy, affable way. "On the contrary, my dear, I think it could be quite a wonderful idea. A useful idea."

Esther stared at him in surprise. Her father always seemed so easygoing and charming, in a sincere and genuine way that made his parish love him, but there was a method to his seemingly relaxed manner, a strategy to his benevolence. She'd seen it in play countless times before, the slightly steely look he got in his eyes even as he gave an easy smile and asked someone to do something—ring the church bells, deliver the parish newsletter, teach Sunday School. It looked effortless, but it required a great deal of skill, and that skill was being used on her, with love and the best intentions, right now.

"Useful?" she repeated cautiously.

"Yes, useful, as long as you don't go rushing into something else." Roger removed his specs to give her a surprisingly frank look.

Esther fought the urge to fidget. "What do you mean, rushing in?" she asked, although she wasn't sure she wanted to know.

"Since you were a little girl, you've always been driven, Esther," Roger said gently. "Determined to be independent. So determined, in fact, that when you were a toddler learning to walk and you fell down and bloodied both your knees, you pushed me away when I tried to comfort you and kept on walking."

Esther managed a small smile, although something twisted inside her at the image. "That sounds like me."

"It does indeed, doesn't it?" Roger smiled in affection. "But you don't need to be so driven all the time, do you, my dear? Because I worry that you will drive yourself right into the ground, or perhaps you will drive yourself to a destination you never expected, and when you look up you'll blink in surprise and sadness to find yourself there."

Esther drew a quick breath, shocked and humbled by his perception. Yes, she had been driven all through school, signing up for a dozen activities, taking four A levels rather than three, and working as hard as she could, all the time, ploughing through essays, exams, everything, her head down, her stride never wavering.

When she'd started at Natural England, she'd been the same, always moving forward. She hadn't been ambitious, not in the usual way, but she'd been determined, just as her father said, to get the job done. To keep going, although where she was going, she didn't think she knew anymore. Maybe she never had. And here she was, just as her father had said, sad and surprised to discover where she'd ended up.

And as for that determination… it had gone along with everything else. All her certainty, all her happiness, all her plans. She felt anchorless and adrift, as if she had nothing, and if she quit her job she wouldn't even have that. Maybe she was crazy to think of it. She needed more in her life, not less, surely?

"I don't think you need to worry, Dad," Esther said. "I can't see myself rushing in to do anything at the moment."

"Let me show you something," Roger said, and rose from his chair. Esther watched in surprise as he left his study. "Come on," he called, and curious and a bit wary, she followed him to the porch where he was yanking on a pair of mud-splattered Welly boots.

"Where are we going?"

"Out."

"Yes, but out where?"

"You'll see."

So Esther put on the Wellies and waxed jacket she'd just taken off, unsure where her father was going, both physically and emotionally. What on earth did he intend on showing her?

It didn't take long to find out. Outside the sun had finally stolen the damp from the air, and clusters of crocuses and snowdrops nestled in the jewel-green grass, tilting their tiny heads to the light.

To Esther's surprise, Roger didn't turn down the church lane towards the village, but rather opened the garden gate and stepped through.

It had been a while since Esther had been in the garden. As a child she'd played there on sunny days, and the church's summer fete had had its tea and cake stand there, and of course her wedding reception had been held there.

She swallowed hard as she remembered standing by the stone wall covered in wisteria, laughing with Will. Feeling happy but, more than that, feeling satisfied. Another box ticked, which was awful, really, wasn't it? Had she been viewing life as nothing more than a checklist to get through?

Roger strode through the garden, past the old rope swing hanging from the horse chestnut tree, the rope now frayed and rotting, to the wooden door in the middle of the stone wall that led to the Victorian walled garden beyond.

Esther had always liked the walled garden; as a child it had reminded her of the story *The Secret Garden*, the vestiges of its heyday now lost amidst the vines and nettles. Through the years, her father had on various occasions tried to do something with it, once even buying a pair of pigs to eat all the nettles, but it had been too big a space and the wild had always claimed it back again.

Now Roger lifted the rusty latch, which screeched in protest, and then pushed open the door on even squeakier hinges.

"What are you doing, Dad?" Esther asked, more curious than wary now. "There's nothing back there."

"On the contrary. I'm showing you something."

"The walled garden? I know it already."

"Yes, I know you do. But I want you to see it with fresh eyes."

They both stepped into the garden, which had gone completely wild, nettles and brambles and weeds growing rampant, covering everything up to about six feet high. Esther couldn't even see the frame of the old glasshouse, its panes missing or broken, that was on the far side, or the stone foundations of the Victorian era cold frames.

"Okay." She leaned against the wall and folded her arms. "I'm seeing it with fresh eyes. Not that there is much to see besides a lot of weeds."

"Exactly." Roger smiled and nodded in approval, as if she'd given the right answer on a quiz. Esther stared at him, baffled.

"Do you know that Thornthwaite has never had an allotment?"

"Yes, the nearest one is Keswick." Esther shrugged.

The residents of the village had long been lobbying for an allotment, but despite the green all around them, there had never been a suitable space. She'd got involved years ago, trying to drum up interest, but it had never taken off and then she'd got busy with work.

"What if you started something?"

Esther stared at him in bemused surprise. "Started something? You mean, make an allotment here?" She glanced at the wild garden, which was about half an acre in size. "It's not big enough, Dad. It could hold maybe two or three plots, max."

"I know that. I'm not talking about an allotment. But what about a community garden, something a bit smaller and friendlier? People could have their own little patches for veg or fruit, perhaps, and then muck in to take care of the rest. You could even donate some of the produce and fruit to the food bank." He nodded towards a few twisty trees, their tops emerging from the brambles. "There are apple and pear, plum and fig, and I think they're all still producing fruit, even if they do need a bit of pruning."

"You're talking about me doing this as a job?" Esther said, still incredulous although she could not deny the tiniest flicker of excitement stirring to life inside her, as if someone had prodded the ashes in her soul and found, to her own surprise, a few glowing embers.

"Not a job precisely," Roger said. "Since I'm not sure there would be any money in it. More of a mission. A reason."

A *reason*. Esther looked away, blinking rapidly. She

hadn't had a reason for a long time, if ever. "I could get some money from the council," she said after a moment. "Maybe. There are grants available for things like this."

"Then you'll do it?"

Again with the flicker, a wary excitement stealing through her, scaring her. Esther took a quick, steadying breath. "I'll think about it," she said.

Chapter Eight

T HE NEXT SATURDAY Esther came downstairs to find her sister Anna sitting at the kitchen table, drinking coffee. Esther stopped in the doorway, nonplussed.

"I came in late last night," Anna explained. "You were already asleep."

"Mum didn't say you were coming," Esther said, although this wasn't strictly true. Her mother might have said, and Esther might not have noticed. Her head had been so full of thoughts the last few days—of her job and the possible redundancy package, of the garden, and of Will.

She couldn't stop thinking about him, wondering what he was doing, how he was feeling, which was both irritating and sad. It had only been a couple of weeks, but she felt like she should be moving on at least a little. "Anyway, welcome home. It's nice to see you."

"Thanks." Anna flashed her a quick smile. "It's nice to see you, too."

"I suppose Mum told you about me and Will?" Esther marched over to the coffeepot, stepping over Charlie who had long ago learned not to bother moving as people stepped around him.

"Er, yes." Anna regarded Esther cautiously over the rim of her mug. "Is that okay?"

"I suppose so." Esther poured herself a coffee and leaned against the counter as she took the first soothing sip. "Everyone's going to learn sooner or later, aren't they?"

"Do you want to talk about it?"

"No."

"Fair enough, then."

Esther regarded her younger sister, aware they hadn't a particularly deep relationship over the years. She was five years older, and she'd always been looking ahead, just as her father had said, too impatient to cast much of a glance behind, which seemed rather awful now. "Sorry," she said after a moment. "I don't mean to sound rude."

Anna gave her the ghost of a smile. "You just sound like your usual self. Maybe a touch pricklier."

Esther gave a small smile, acknowledging the point. "Should I be offended by that?"

"I don't know."

"You seem happier," Esther said abruptly. Anna had always been the shy, quiet one, content to blend into the background and be forgotten. Anna had starting dating her father's new curate, Simon, over Christmas, and judging by the frequency of her visits back to Thornthwaite, it looked to be fairly serious.

"I am happy," Anna said quietly. "And not just happier, because I don't think I actually was before."

"Weren't you?" Esther sat down at the table and cradled her mug between her hands, savouring the warmth. "Why not?"

Anna shrugged. "It's not very exciting, just to exist."

"Is that what you were doing?"

"More or less."

Esther took a sip of coffee. "That sounds rather grim."

Anna managed a small smile back. "It does, doesn't it?"

The ensuing silence made Esther wonder. Was she in the same boat as her sister? Had life become about nothing more than existence? That was what it had felt like since that awful ultrasound, and maybe even before that, long before that. Slogging through the days. Not seeing the point to anything, even her marriage, as she kept plodding towards an endpoint that probably didn't even exist... just as Anna seemed to have been doing.

Why did they all have to be so bloody buttoned-up, with loving parents and a stable home life? Was it simply a part of being British, or were they all still lingering in the shadow of Jamie's death? Or maybe, Esther acknowledged with a tired sigh, they were just made that way.

"I'm sorry about you and Will, Esther," Anna said quietly, and she managed a nod.

"Thank you. I'm glad things are going well between you and Simon." All her sisters seemed to have found happiness and sorted their lives out now, except for her. Anna was with Simon, Rachel was getting married, and Miriam, the baby of the family, was living it up in Australia. Esther sighed, trying not to feel envious of how they'd managed life's storms and struggles better than she had.

"They are." Anna's smile was both shy and proud, and really quite lovely.

Esther felt a pang of compassion; she'd known, in the periphery of her mind, that Anna had been having a hard time of it over the years, with her shyness and anxiety. Sometimes Esther had been exasperated or impatient with her sister's difficulties; other times she'd been sympathetic, if from a distance.

"Do you think you'll move back to Thornthwaite, then?" she asked.

"Well, it's early days yet," Anna answered, blushing. "We've only been dating for three months."

"True, but you must think about it. He'll be living in the vicarage…" Simon would be taking over from her father when her parents moved to China at the end of July. It was something Esther still couldn't let herself think about too much. Didn't want to imagine.

"It's strange." Anna's soft gaze swept over the familiar kitchen, taking in all its lovably shabby cosiness, from the old Aga that broke at least once a year, usually at an incredibly inconvenient time like Christmas Eve, to Charlie snoozing in front of it; the mismatched chairs painted bright colours, the jumble of dishes in the pantry, also mismatched. "I can't imagine Mum and Dad not here."

"I wish they wouldn't go." As soon as she'd blurted the words, Esther wished she hadn't. She sounded like such a child, a baby. And she felt like one. She hadn't realized until that moment quite how much she would miss her parents. Quite how much she wanted them in her life, especially now, when everything felt so uncertain. When she felt empty.

"So do I," Anna answered softly. "But I understand why they are."

"Do you? China…" Esther shook her head. "It's so far, and we're all here, except for Miriam."

"Dad's been here a long time. Maybe he needs a change, a challenge."

"Can you see Mum in China, though?" Esther asked frankly. Her mother was happiest in the vicarage, baking and making cups of tea, welcoming visitors, always busy and smiling. "Because I can't." As she said it, she realized how much it was true. She couldn't see her mother in China at all.

"Mum will be fine," Anna said firmly, surprising Esther a little with how sure she sounded. "She's strong."

"Yes, I suppose." She took another sip of now-lukewarm coffee. "But that makes it sound like something to be endured, doesn't it? To be got through." Anna looked uncertain and Esther decided not to pursue the line of thought. She'd been feeling like life was something to be endured right here in Thornthwaite. "I'll miss them, though."

"I know. Even when I didn't come home very often, I knew they were here." Anna's lips trembled as she tried for a smile. "And that made a big difference."

"Yes, it did." Even though she'd only lived a few miles away, Esther hadn't come back to the vicarage, save for her mother's regular Sunday roast dinners. Even so, just like Anna, knowing her parents were here and always willing to listen or help had made a big difference. "Right." She rose from the table and put her mug in the dishwasher. "I should crack on."

"Are you working?" Anna asked. "It's Saturday."

"No, I just have a few things to do." Esther wanted to take a proper look at the walled garden. In the five days since her father had suggested the community garden idea, she'd rolled it around in her mind, veering between excitement, terror, and a dismissive certainty that it could never work, that she shouldn't even try.

She hadn't gone out to the garden again, hadn't wanted to tempt herself with something that was probably impossible. But yesterday afternoon an email had come back from the head office responding to her tentative email query with a potential redundancy package that was surprisingly generous. It almost felt like fate, or, as her parents would say, Providence. She hadn't responded yet, though. Hadn't dared to dream.

"What are you up to today?" Esther asked Anna, whose sudden smile was like a ray of sunshine.

"Simon and I are going to go rambling."

"I didn't think you were much of a hiker," Esther remarked, and Anna shrugged, still smiling.

"Needs must, and I'd be happy doing anything with Simon."

Esther felt another pang of envy; Anna's happiness seemed so simple, so untarnished and pure. Why did everything have to feel so complicated with her? But she wasn't going to think about that now. She wasn't going to think about Will or her job or the bleakness of everything that sometimes felt like a weight on top of her chest, making it hard to breathe, never mind actually do anything. No, for a little while she was going to lose herself in the possibilities of a walled garden.

The day was sunny with a hint of spring-like warmth as Esther opened the door into the walled garden, feeling a bit like Mary Lennox in *The Secret Garden*, poking about the overgrown vines and brambles, discovering the magic of it for the first time.

The garden looked just as wild and unmanageable as it had a few days ago when she'd viewed it with her father, or even more so, now that she was regarding the space with a more discerning eye. It was more *Sleeping Beauty* than *Secret Garden,* a hundred years of thorns and brambles covering everything. The wilderness was so impenetrable that she couldn't take much more than a step forward, but this time Esther was prepared.

She reached for the large pair of secateurs she'd brought and started cutting a path out of the bramble one snip at a time. It was slow, tiring work; what she really needed was some sort of cultivator or tiller, or even a backhoe, although that wouldn't fit through the gate. But since she didn't have any of those and she wanted to have a look around, secateurs it was.

It took her the better part of an hour just to make the tiniest of dents in the wilderness, but it was enough to get a sense of the place. Standing on top of a fallen log in the middle of the garden, a sea of bramble all around her, Esther could make out the glasshouse, covered in bindweed, and just about glimpse the foundation of the Victorian cold frames. Her mind started to wander, and then to race.

The glasshouse needed a bit of TLC, but it was big enough to grow orange trees along with tomatoes and cucumbers, and any other plants that couldn't survive Cumbria's harsh climes. Besides the little orchard, which had a half dozen twisty trees, there was space for several good-sized veg plots, and perhaps even a decorative section as well, with chairs and tables, a communal outdoor space to have coffee mornings or concerts...

For a second, Esther could almost imagine it—the sun shining, people milling around, sitting in chairs or working their plots. She started to smile.

The sun had gone behind a bank of clouds and there was the damp smell of rain in the air, so Esther climbed down from the log and headed back to the vicarage, her step slowing when she saw the familiar battered and muddy Land Rover in the drive, next to her own. *Will.* What was he doing here?

Hope and fear tangled in her chest as she resumed walking towards the front door, only to have it open before she'd touched the knob. Will stood there, looking rumpled and tired and rather wonderful, his blue eyes widening in shock when he caught sight of her.

"I thought you were out."

"I was in the garden."

His eyes narrowed. "The garden?"

"What are you doing here?" Esther asked, mainly to ward off any questions about the garden. She wasn't ready to tell anyone about her fragile, barely-there plans.

"Your mum asked me to fix the downstairs loo." Will had always been her parents' informal handyman, but Esther thought they could have called someone else this once, considering the situation.

"Oh." They regarded each other for a few tense seconds. "Is it fixed?"

"Not yet. I was just going out to get a wrench."

"Right." She sidled past him, taking off her boots and coat, feeling uneasy and hyperaware of Will's presence. A few moments later he came back inside armed with a wrench and, knowing it was what her mother would do, Esther asked, "Would you like a cuppa?"

"Wouldn't mind," Will said, brushing past her into the bathroom.

Feeling a bit woebegone and not wanting to figure out why, Esther retreated to the kitchen.

>>><<<

HE SHOULD HAVE said no to Ruth Holley when she'd asked him to look at the loo, Will reflected darkly as he started taking the thing apart, conscious of Esther moving about in the kitchen, only one thin wall—the downstairs loo was a later addition, carved out of the study—between them. But he hadn't said no, hadn't even thought of it, because Ruth was still his mother-in-law and the vicarage still felt like his second home, even if Esther—his wife—didn't want him anywhere near it.

For the last week he'd tortured himself by remembering her set, grim expression when she'd spelled it out for him. *I don't want your baby. Ever.*

He should have clued in when she'd walked out on him so precipitously. She was done with him, had been done for a long time. Why hadn't he seen it? And really, why had he been surprised? He'd always felt lucky, landing Esther. A bloke like him, without much to say, having kept his head down most of his life. He'd been amazed she'd looked twice at him.

"Tea." Will glanced back to see Esther standing in the doorway of the bathroom, bearing a mug of tea.

"Thanks," he said gruffly, half-wishing he hadn't agreed to a cuppa, but knowing he did because not to had seemed churlish, childish, as if he was having a strop simply because she didn't like him anymore. He always had a cuppa. It was practically a family joke, except he didn't even know if this was his family anymore, and that hurt him as much as anything else.

He'd lost his own family when he'd been nineteen, out of both tragedy and then his own stupidity, and when the Holleys had welcomed him as their own he'd felt part of something bigger than himself, for the first time in years. Too many years. And now he felt the lack, the nothingness, all the more. He really was alone.

Esther took a step into the bathroom and Will scooted up and held out a hand. "Thanks," he said again, taking the mug. She remained where she was, although Will had expected her to go. He looked away, because he didn't want to see the expression on her face, whatever it was. Resignation, impatience, contempt? Hatred?

Anger fizzed through him at the memory of those awful words. *I didn't want your baby.*

"Will, I'm thinking of giving up my job."

He turned quickly towards her, tea sloshing out of his mug. "You mean quitting?"

"Taking one of those redundancy packages." Esther twisted her hands together, looking uncharacteristically nervous. "You remember when they were offering them a few years ago?"

"Yes…" Vaguely. Esther hadn't considered it for a moment. "But you love your job."

"I used to," Esther corrected. "I haven't for a while."

Something else he hadn't known. Something else she'd kept from him. Will looked away.

"So I thought I might take it," Esther said, her voice wavering. "But I also thought you should know, because… well, because I know my salary wasn't all that much, but it was still something…"

It took him a few seconds to realize what she was implying. "I don't need your money, Esther."

"I know things are tight on the farm…"

Will's chest hurt with an unbearable ache. He turned back to the loo, wanting to focus on something he knew he could fix. "I don't need your money," he said again, his voice low. "I don't want it."

He expected her to leave then, but she didn't. She simply stood, her hands twisted together, her expression tense and unhappy, while he tried not to look at her and failed.

"How are things at the farm?" she asked eventually, and Will let out a huff of disbelieving sound. Why was she bothering to ask?

"They're fine."

"And... Toby?"

Toby? She cared about their dog, but not him? Of course, fair enough, he'd been little more than a pup when they'd got together. "He's fine, too. Slowing down a bit, but he has for a while." He reached for a wrench, determined to concentrate on his work, and eventually, after what felt like an age, Esther tiptoed away.

Will let out a sigh, whether of relief or resignation he couldn't say. He felt both. He felt too much, sadness swamping him that after ten years together, it had come to this, and he still wasn't sure he really understood why.

Chapter Nine

THE NEXT MORNING Esther woke up to the pealing of the church bells and the distant sounds of her family getting ready for the morning service. She lay in bed and listened to the pipes protest and rumble as someone took a shower, and then heard Anna call something to their mother. They were all going, of course, Anna too. Esther was the only one who was staying at home, feeling miserable after that awful, awkward conversation with Will.

She remembered the dark, narrowed look he'd given her, almost as if he hated her now, or even worse, that he was indifferent—or perhaps just trying to be. Either way, it made her insides writhe and sink with misery, even as she acknowledged he had every reason to hate her after what she'd said. What she'd felt. Nothing could make up for that.

Sighing, Esther rose from bed and dressed, determined to keep busy today, which would at least keep her from thinking. She ate a quick breakfast before gathering garden tools from the shed in the little courtyard behind the kitchen and then headed out to the walled garden.

The sight of it both invigorated and intimidated her; the space she'd cleared yesterday was smaller than she'd remembered, the wild of brambles, weeds, and nettles taller and thicker, as well. She felt like Prince Phillip in *Sleeping Beauty*, hacking his way through the thorns. She didn't know who or what was the evil fairy in that scenario, but she decided not to examine it too closely. Not to examine anything, because the point of getting out here under a pale blue sky, the air fresh, the earth damp and crumbly underneath her feet, was not to think. To take a break from her brain, which frankly felt rather wonderful.

And it was wonderful, to get dirty and sweaty, accomplishing something, seeing the pile of garden waste grow bigger by the gate. Perhaps they could have a bonfire. She was so busy cutting and hacking that she didn't hear the creak of the gate or anyone approach until Anna called out, "Hey, don't go too crazy!"

Esther looked up, blinking her sister and Simon into focus. A droplet of sweat fell into her eye and she swiped her forehead with her arm. "I've barely made a start." She glanced around at the garden, which was still about ninety-eight percent bramble.

"What are you doing out here, though?" Anna asked, her eyes crinkling with concern. "This has always been nothing but bramble, except for when Dad got those pigs—do you remember?" She turned to Simon with a smile. "We called them Romeo and Juliet, although, actually, I think they were both sows. They ate everything, but the smell of them bothered the neighbours on the other side of the garden." She nodded towards a couple of converted barn cottages whose slanting roofs were visible above the far wall of the garden. "So Dad had them carted off to the abattoir. Rachel cried, as I remember. She'd got quite attached to them."

"We had bacon and sausage for a year, though," Esther reminded her, and Anna let out a peal of laughter.

"Yes, and that's what Dad called them both, wasn't it?" She turned back to Simon, her eyes alight. "We called them Romeo and Juliet, and he called them Bacon and Sausage. Horrible." But she was laughing, and Esther found herself smiling at the memory, even as it tugged a deep place inside her that she hadn't accessed in a long time. Jamie had been alive then. He'd been the one to call them Bacon and Sausage first. Ruth had tsked-tsked but Roger had thought it clever and amusing.

Her heart gave a sudden, surprising wrench as the memory gained an almost crystalline clarity; for a second, Esther felt as if she could walk right into it, take up where they'd left off twenty years ago, when things had felt simple and happy, and she... what had she felt? Lighter, perhaps. Less driven.

"Esther," Anna said, and it felt as if she were calling from far away. "Esther, are you coming?"

Esther blinked both her sister and Simon back into focus; Simon was looking at her with gentle, frowning concern.

"Sorry, what?"

"Are you coming inside?" Anna asked, and Esther could tell it was not the first time she'd made the invitation. "Rachel and Dan are here, and Mum's doing a roast, due to Simon."

Simon rolled his eyes. "You mean due to you being here all the way from Manchester. I'm old hat already."

Anna gave him a teasing look and linked arms with him, and Esther watched them in a mixture of envy and happiness for her sister. They were both clearly smitten, and she was glad for them.

"So?" Anna raised her eyebrows and Esther realized she was still staring, saying nothing. "Are you coming? I need to do the Yorkshire puds. Don't you do the green veg usually?"

"Yes. And make the custard for the pudding." Both had been her jobs since she'd been about nine, and judged old enough for the responsibility.

"You know how we all have different jobs for a Sunday roast?" Anna said to Simon, and he smiled down at her, his hazel eyes full of affection.

"You might have told me once or twice."

"Sorry." Anna let out an embarrassed laugh. "Family traditions are important, that's all."

"Very important," Simon agreed, and they started walking back towards the vicarage. Esther propped the pair of shears she'd been using to hack through the undergrowth against the wall and then carefully closed the garden gate.

"So what are you doing back there, Esther?" Simon asked conversationally as they made their way across the lawn to the front of the vicarage.

Esther hesitated, a vaguely unwelcome realization trickling through her. In less than four months, Simon would be moving into the vicarage as vicar, taking over from her father when her parents moved to China. It still all seemed so incredible that Esther couldn't quite believe it was happening that soon. And when Simon did move into the vicarage, he would of course be in charge of the property, including the garden. Meaning she needed his permission for her community garden scheme, something she hadn't considered until now.

"Actually," she began, "I'm thinking of starting a community garden. My father gave me the idea," she clarified quickly. "We never really did anything with the walled garden in all the years we've lived here. But of course you might want to do something with it..." She trailed off, realizing she was putting him in a rather uncomfortable position of having to say yes or feeling mean for saying no.

"A community garden seems like a fantastic idea," Simon said easily. They'd reached the front steps of the vicarage and he held the door open for both her and Anna. "I'm certainly not planning to do anything with that space. I'll have enough to do, keeping the grass mowed here." He gestured to the expanse of garden they'd just walked through. "What kind of community garden? Veg and fruit, or flowers..."

"A bit of everything, really. Whatever people want to do, once they get stuck in."

"So how come you're clearing it by yourself?" Simon asked. "If it's a community project?"

Esther stared at him gormlessly for a moment as a flush fought its way up her face. That was a very good question. A community garden was one that was worked by the community. Clearing it, planning it—everything should be done by the people of Thornthwaite, not Esther Langley alone.

"I'm just at the assessing stage right now," she said, wincing at how pompous she sounded. "To see if the land is viable."

Simon nodded, looking suitably impressed. "That sounds like a plan."

It wasn't, not really, and Esther's thoughts circled fruitlessly as she went into the kitchen to do her part for the roast dinner. How was she going to get the community involved? How was any of this going to *work?*

"You want to do the veg?" Ruth looked both surprised and pleased when Esther volunteered, which made her feel both guilty and the tiniest bit annoyed. All right, yes, she'd been moping around, doing basically nothing, for three whole weeks, but it had only been three weeks. She'd been making the green veg and custard for Sunday dinners for over twenty-five years before that.

"It is my job, isn't it?" Esther answered, trying to sound light, and almost managing it. She opened the fridge. "What should we have? Broccoli or brussels sprouts?"

"You choose, darling."

Her mother sounded so pathetically pleased that Esther was finally taking an interest in anything other than her own navel that Esther winced with remorse. "Broccoli, it is." She took out the head of broccoli from the fridge and starting chopping it into florets while her mum moved about and Anna came in to put the Yorkshire puddings into the oven.

Rachel came in soon after to check on the roast potatoes, which had always been her brief, and Esther could hear Roger's tones of jovial bonhomie from the hall, along with the murmuring replies of Dan and Simon. His job was to pour the sherry, something he did with both alacrity and enthusiasm.

There was a chaotic symmetry to the women's movements around the kitchen, dancing and dodging out of the way, holding hot pans aloft as they stepped over Charlie, who stubbornly insisted on remaining prostrate in front of the Aga despite the activity all around him. Mouthwatering smells wafted through the kitchen and the whole house, of sizzling roast pork and the sweet scent of applesauce.

As Esther put the broccoli on to boil, timing it perfectly with the Yorkshires needing ten minutes to go, Roger came in, holding high the familiar indigo bottle of Bristol Cream. "Pre-dinner sherry, anyone?"

Everyone chorused yes and Esther leaned against the counter, watching her father pour, a benevolent smile on his face. She found her own gaze moving around the room restlessly, and, with a jolt, she realized who she was looking for, lounging in the corner, giving her a slow smile across the steamy haze of a busy kitchen. But of course Will wasn't there, and maybe never would be again, a possibility which sent something close to terror lurching through her. Will belonged here, even if he didn't belong with her. It was a tangle, impossible thought.

It was almost as if her father was attuned to what she was thinking because he gave her a compassionate smile as he handed her a thimble's worth of sherry. "Will's more of a bitter man, isn't he?"

"You know he is, Dad." Esther murmured her thanks as she took a sip of the sweet sherry.

"How is he?" Ruth asked quietly. "How's he managing on the farm?"

"Fine, I think." With an uncomfortable lurch Esther realized how many relationships she'd unintentionally severed when she'd walked out of Will's house several weeks ago. As their only son-in-law, Will had always got on well with her parents, and sometimes Esther wondered if he felt a little bit like the son they'd lost, come home again. Did they miss him as much as she did?

But of course she couldn't let herself miss him. It was too late for that. Far, far too late, thanks to everything she'd done and said.

"I think it's all ready," Ruth announced brightly, and the

next few minutes were spent rushing serving dishes to the table while Roger made a big production of carving the pork, all in the hope of things being at least mostly lukewarm by the time they said grace.

They sat around the table, joining hands as her parents had insisted ever since Esther and her siblings were small, suffering through the childhood years of squirming and insisting the person next to them had wiped their nose on their hand, which they very well might have done.

Roger took a moment, their hands all linked, to gaze around the table, managing to seem both solemn and smiling. Esther's throat caught and she tried to return his look steadily, not wanting to betray how raw she still felt about everything. How fragile. "For what we are about to receive, may we be truly grateful."

"Amen," everyone chorused, Esther murmuring the word, and then Ruth started passing dishes around as people loaded up their plates. It was all so convivial and cheerful, and it made Esther feel both happy and sad. She'd taken these dinners for granted for a long time. In fact, if she was brutally honest, which she usually was, she'd found them a bit tedious at times; her father's bonhomie the tiniest bit grating, her mother's concerned kindliness a little much. Esther was such a *cow* sometimes, thinking that way. She hated it about herself, hated it with a vicious passion, and yet she didn't know how to change.

"So Esther was telling me a little bit about the community garden project," Simon said as he placed a perfectly golden and puffy Yorkshire pudding on his plate. "Sounds interesting."

"Subject to your approval, of course," Roger returned, in a tone that suggested he knew this would not be in question.

"You know I'm behind anything that gets the community on church land," Simon joked. "Of course, through the doors would be even better!"

"Wouldn't it just."

Esther tried not to squirm as she considered her lack of attendance over the last twelve years, save for the high holidays.

"So tell us about it, Esther," Simon invited, and she shrugged, uneasy and uncertain, and so unlike her old self, the self she'd carefully constructed over the years which seemed to be falling apart a little more every day.

"I think I've told you the gist. I'm not sure there's much more."

"Will you apply for grants from the council, that sort of thing?"

"I need to look into it, but, yes, I should think so…"

"And what about getting people involved?" Simon continued, looking decidedly interested. "How do you plan to drum up interest?"

"Umm…" Esther stared at him helplessly.

Her old self, the one who had been married and certain about everything, would have given him a smart and perhaps terse answer, so sure of what she would do, how she would do it, and how she would succeed. But somehow, in the last few weeks and months, that certain Esther had disappeared. Esther had no idea if she'd find her again… or if she even wanted to. She wasn't sure she'd liked her all that much, really. But who on earth was she supposed to be instead?

"I have an idea," Roger chimed in. "Why don't you come to the coffee morning this Wednesday and do a little presentation?"

Esther goggled at him. "A presentation?"

"Why not? You could knock one up on your laptop in your sleep."

"For the ten steps to joining our new environmental scheme, perhaps," Esther returned a little tartly. "But I've barely thought about this, Dad."

"You've been out in the garden a fair bit," Roger returned reasonably.

"Yes, but…" Going out in the garden had more about clearing her head, or perhaps filling it, than anything else. It had been a much-needed escape from thinking about Will, and the baby-that-wasn't, and everything that had gone wrong with her life. It had kept her from thinking about the emptiness she felt in the heart of herself, an emptiness she was afraid to examine too closely, or even at all.

"And," Roger continued in the same, reasonable tone, "you have till Wednesday to work something up. Ten a.m. it starts. How about you give a little talk at half past?"

Her father was a master at this sort of thing. How many times in church had Esther overheard her father jovially inviting someone to teach Sunday School or serve as a sidesman, gently ignoring their blustering attempts to put him off, and pencilling them in before they'd managed a proper answer? She knew better than to protest, and, in any case, the garden gave her a purpose when she badly needed one. Taking the next step, however intimidating it felt, was logical.

The conversation drifted on to Rachel and Dan's wedding, and the planned trip to Manchester in a few weeks to try on bridesmaid dresses.

Anna and Ruth rose to clear plates, and Simon and Dan started to help as Esther went to get the custard for the apple crumble.

Later, as she helped her mother and sisters in the kitchen, her father having retreated to his study, she wondered what she would say to the friendly pensioners who made up ninety percent of coffee morning attendees. Would they really be interested in a community garden? And if they were, what if it became a huge mess, like anything in a village did, with too many people wanting different things, and even more people trying to be in charge?

Esther had never been a people person, not like her parents or Rachel. She wouldn't know how to handle something like that. Logistics she could manage, but people? Feelings? She'd done a pretty poor job so far.

And yet… Esther hung the damp dish towel over the Aga rail as Ruth switched on the kettle, the dishes done, the vicarage easing into the relaxed warmth of a Sunday afternoon.

She wanted to do this, scared as she was. At least part of her did. Part of her recognized the need for a change, for a chance. And maybe, just maybe, this could be it.

Chapter Ten

ESTHER POKED HER head around the door of the church hall, blinking in the steamy fug of a room filled with people and boiling kettles. The excited chatter of about three dozen people seemed to fall to a buzzy hum as everyone caught sight of Esther. Recalcitrant vicar's daughter, suddenly appearing at a church function. Wonders were not ceasing, it seemed. The Red Sea had just peeled back its waters yet again.

"Esther!" Mary Bell, a comfortable woman with a wide smile and a tight grey perm beckoned her over to a table laden with homemade cakes. "What can I get you? Black Forest, Victoria sponge, lemon drizzle, coffee walnut..."

"Oh, wow." Esther gazed down at the display of cakes. "They all look delicious." She couldn't remember the last time she'd been to a coffee morning. As a child, she'd always gone across during half-terms and holidays, mainly for the free cake. Donations of a pound fifty were requested but as the vicar's children they'd always had a free pass. And the cakes were delicious. But it had been many years, at least fifteen, since she'd even been in this hall, never mind at a coffee morning. It felt odd to be back, amidst the familiar and strangely comforting scents of wet coats, instant coffee, and a faint, lingering aroma of sweaty socks, no doubt from the nights the Cubs used the hall.

"Well?" Mary smiled at her, and Esther thought she detected a trace of sympathy in the elderly woman's crinkled eyes. She knew about Will, of course. Nothing stayed private in Thornthwaite, especially when your father was the vicar. Everyone in this room probably knew, and she was meant to talk to them all in twenty minutes.

"I'll have the coffee walnut," Esther said finally, the words coming out in something almost like a gasp. The space between her shoulder blades prickled and her palms felt clammy. There might have only been thirty or forty people in the hall, but she felt as if a thousand eyes were boring into her back.

Mary handed her a generous slice on a small plate with a paper napkin. "It's nice to see you, Esther," she said warmly.

"Thanks," Esther murmured, and then, bracing herself, turned to face the crowd. No one was actually looking at her, but it felt as if they were. She felt as if the crowded aisle between the folding tables and chairs was a catwalk, and she was in the spotlight. Slowly she inched her way down it, dodging knitting bags and coats draped over chairs, to finally squeeze into an empty space at the end of a long table.

She put her cake down and glanced up at the tableful of

pensioners, most of them having stopped their animated conversation to inspect her, some, she realized with a sinking sensation, in a not altogether friendly fashion.

"Er… hello," she said, trying for a smile. Everyone knew her, had seen her in nappies, with braces, with pimples, when she'd gone through an unfortunate Goth phase in uni. They'd watched her grow up, and she barely knew their names. In fact, she *didn't* know their names. The realization was humbling as well as a bit shaming.

"How are you getting on then, Esther?" asked a woman with beady eyes and a brisk look to her. "Still working all hours for the environment?"

"Just the usual nine to five, really." Esther couldn't tell if the woman had sounded sniffy or merely abrupt. She crumbled a bit of cake with the tines of her fork.

"And how's that husband of yours? Bringing the lambs in?"

"Yes, I think so."

Eyes around the table narrowed. "You think so?" repeated the woman who Esther was desperately trying to place.

Churchgoer? Or just someone around the village? That was the trouble; everyone knew her, and she definitely didn't know everyone.

"I mean, I'm sure he is," Esther returned, her voice turning a touch too strident. She felt as she did when she walked into the sea and the sandy bottom suddenly gave way, leaving her flailing. Coughing and choking too, if she'd inhaled a mouthful of salt water.

And then she did inhale, not salt water but cake, having popped a bite into her mouth to forestall having to answer any more questions, and then promptly starting to choke, because it seemed she wasn't capable of anything anymore.

Someone went to fetch a glass of water while a kindly woman with milky eyes and a vague smile patted her on the back and Esther sprayed the table with coffee-walnut crumbs.

"Sorry about that," she gasped out a few minutes later when she'd taken a couple sips of water and managed, with quite a lot of effort, to get her coughing fit under control. "Sorry," she said again. Thankfully most of the table had resumed their earlier conversations, leaving only the beady-eyed woman staring her down across ten feet of fake wood.

"You're living at the vicarage now, then?"

Conversations that had just started up went silent. Esther fought the urge to say something rude, or worse, to cry. "Yes," she said, dabbing at cake crumbs with the tip of her finger. "I am. For a little bit."

The door to the hall opened and her father appeared on a gust of wind, his cheeks reddened by cold, his manner as jovial as ever. His arrival thankfully distracted Beady Eyes from continuing her determined inquisition, and Esther was sorely tempted to slope off, never mind her planned little announcement. She'd spent all yesterday evening toying with a slick Power Point presentation only to realize how ridiculous it was. Thornthwaite coffee mornings didn't do Power Point. Most of the people sipping tea and nibbling cake probably didn't even have email.

"Ah, there she is!" Her father's voice boomed across the room and Esther tried not to squirm. "Friends, my lovely daughter Esther has a little announcement to make. I hope you'll give her your full attention."

Roger sent her a look full of affection and love, his smile beaming full-watt encouragement, so much so Esther couldn't actually blame him for putting her in the spotlight so precipitously, as much as she wanted to.

Her father raised his eyebrows. "Esther?"

"Right." She cleared her throat, her heart starting to thud. This shouldn't be so nerve-wracking. She'd given talks to colleagues, waxed on and on for farmers. She was a confident, forthright person. At least, she used to be. Now she didn't know who she was anymore, and everyone was waiting for her to speak. "So, umm…"

"Speak up!" This from a gruff old man with his flat cap pulled down low, his arms folded across his chest.

"Why don't you come to the front, dear?" Mary Bell suggested, and with a quick nod and a gulp Esther made her way forward. The room was completely silent, save for the low-grade hiss of the kettle and the occasional creak of a chair.

"Okay," Esther murmured, and once again she edged her way between the tables to the front of the room. Turned around. Took a breath. And her mind went blank.

It had never happened to her before; it was as if someone had pressed delete in her brain. Nothing remained. She, Esther Langley, confident, self-assured, strident woman, was left gaping and speechless.

"Well, then?" someone barked, and this was followed by a theatrical whisper.

"Oh, hush up, Frank, and let the girl have a moment."

"Esther?" Her father's voice was gentle and full of concern. "Love?"

The tenderness in his voice somehow managed to kickstart her brain. Sort of.

"Right. Garden." She blurted the two words while everyone looked on, bemused. "That is, I'm thinking of starting a community garden, available to everyone, managed by everyone." She took a deep breath as her stuttering heart rate started to even out. "For everyone." She blinked the sea of faces into focus and saw that, for the most part, everyone was looking at her with friendly interest, their smiles as encouraging as her father's.

Heartened, Esther continued, her voice growing in strength and conviction. She could do this. She was doing it. And so carefully, her voice growing stronger, she outlined her plan, admitting the parts she didn't know, trying her best to paint a vision of a beautiful, welcoming space for the people of Thornthwaite, and definitely avoiding the mocking little voice in the back of her head that hissed at her to pipe down, because she had no idea what she was doing.

"That was wonderful, darling," Roger said once she'd finished and left a sheet for people who were interested in knowing more to sign.

"Thanks, Dad." Esther let out a shaky laugh; now that it was over she was feeling the post-adrenalin rush and a bit ridiculous for it. It wasn't as if she'd given a speech to hundreds of people. She'd made an announcement to the Thornthwaite coffee morning, for goodness' sake, about thirty pensioners, most of whom had seen her wet her pants in church when she'd been four years old. "I don't know why I was so nervous."

"You've had a knock," Roger said quietly. "Perhaps a few. It can make things like this feel like scaling Mount Everest."

"I know, but…" For a second Esther wanted to tell him how lost she felt, as if she didn't know herself anymore. She wanted to explain that it was this alarming emptiness at the heart of herself that had made her leave Will, but she didn't know if that even made sense. Nothing did. "Thanks, Dad," she said instead, and he smiled and squeezed her shoulder.

A few moments later, just as Esther was hoping to make her escape, she was accosted by the youngest person in the room, save for herself. It took her a moment to place the face—dark hair, dimples. Mark Taylor, the music teacher.

"Do you make a habit of coming to coffee mornings?" she said, bemused, and he grinned and spread his hands.

"The cake is very good."

"Yes, it is." They appraised each other for a few seconds while Esther tried not to feel uneasy. "Look, I'll come straight to the point. Your sister mentioned you'd separated from your husband and I was wondering if you'd like to go out for a drink."

"Oh." Esther's mind buzzed with shock. No matter how friendly Mark Taylor was, she still hadn't quite been expecting that. She'd been separated from Will only for three weeks. "Um…"

"Just as friends," Mark said quickly. "I know the separation is recent. But I thought, you know, maybe you could use a friend."

She could, but a friend who was a single male and certainly charming as well as attractive? Esther's unease deepened. It felt too much like a date, and yet…

"Only if you want to," Mark added. He looked like he was beginning to regret his invitation, and for some reason that made Esther blurt, "No, I would. It's so kind of you to ask. I've been in what feels like an isolation tank for the last few weeks, so… yes. Thanks." They made hasty, awkward arrangements to meet at The Queen's Sorrow on Friday night, and then Esther was walking out into the fresh spring air; her father had promised to pick up the signup sheet when the coffee morning was over.

"How did it go?" Ruth asked as soon as Esther came through the vicarage door.

"Fine, I think. Why weren't you there, Mum?" Esther asked curiously as she came into the kitchen. "Don't you usually go to the coffee mornings?" Armed with several cakes.

"Yes, but..." Ruth shrugged. "I didn't want you to feel like we were ganging up on you."

"Ganging up..." Esther sank into a chair. "I wouldn't have felt that way."

"I'm glad." Ruth did her usual thing of bustling about the kitchen, although Esther couldn't see there was much to do. She wiped an already clean counter and moved a few mugs around. "I just didn't want you to feel pressured somehow. Anyway." She turned back to Esther with a bright smile. "How did it go? Tell me all about it."

So Esther did, sparing no details, not even her cake-spraying episode, and was rewarded by sending her mother into gales of laughter, so much so that she found she was laughing too, and what had seemed fairly mortifying half an hour ago now was rather hilarious. And, Esther realized, it felt good to laugh, like exercising a muscle that had started to atrophy.

"I don't think I've laughed like this in ages," she said, once they'd both subsided. "My stomach muscles hurt."

"So do mine, or what little stomach muscle I have left, after five children." Ruth sighed and leaned back against the chair. "It feels good, though, doesn't it?"

"It does." Esther regarded her mother for a moment.

"Mum," she asked, "do you really want to go to China?"

Ruth blinked, clearly surprised by the sudden switch. "What makes you ask that?"

"I don't know… I suppose because you seem so happy here."

Ruth glanced down at the kitchen table, tracing the pattern in the grain of wood with her fingers. "I have been happy here," she admitted quietly. "Of course I have. But that doesn't mean I can't be happy somewhere else."

"But do you *want* to go to China?" Esther asked, leaning forward, feeling a sudden need to press the point.

Ruth looked up with a weary smile. "Esther, after seven years of marriage, don't you know the answer to that?"

"What?" She blinked, confused. This wasn't about her.

"I want to go to China," Ruth said simply, "because your father wants to go to China. And if you're thinking of trotting out some tired feminist principles, please don't. This isn't about bending my will to a man's. It's about marriage, and what it means."

Esther stared at her for a moment, trying to sift through all she'd said, and all she hadn't. "So you don't really want to go," she said after a moment, and Ruth gave an exasperated harrumph.

"That wasn't what I was saying at all. And if you think it was, you've missed the point entirely."

Chastened, Esther stayed silent. Maybe she had missed the point… in a lot of ways. Was there some lesson her mum was trying to impart to her that related to her and Will? It made Esther squirm inside to consider it.

"But what if," she finally burst out, "you go to China and you don't like it and you're not happy? What if making Dad happy isn't enough?"

Ruth frowned at her, her gaze searching. "Why do I feel as if we're not talking about China anymore?"

Because they weren't. With a gulp, Esther blurted, "I didn't want to have a baby."

Ruth blinked slowly, her eyes wide with shock. Esther instantly regretted her admission.

"But… why not?"

"Plenty of people don't want to have children, Mum." She couldn't look at her as she said it.

"You don't want to have children? Any children?" Esther shrugged, still not meeting her mum's eyes. "You never said anything about it."

"I suppose I didn't quite realize."

"But Will knows?"

Esther looked up with a rather grim smile. "He knows now."

Ruth gave Esther a hard stare, the kind she'd been subjected to as a child, when her mother had known she'd done something wrong but wasn't sure what. "Are you saying he didn't know before? When you were pregnant?"

Esther swallowed hard. She was starting to wish she hadn't brought all this up. "No," she admitted in a low voice. "He didn't."

"Esther, is this why you've separated? Because Will wants children and you don't?"

"No… not exactly."

"Then why?"

"Because we weren't making each other happy."

"I think you were making Will happy," Ruth said tartly. "I'm quite sure he would say that."

Feeling cornered now, Esther became a bit reckless. "Fine," she said. "Then he wasn't making me happy."

"I'm not sure it's the job of a spouse to make one happy," Ruth replied, "but I won't belabour that particular point now. Didn't you think counselling might help? Something?"

"There was no point."

Ruth shook her head. "No point? Esther, can you honestly say you're happier, happy at all, now, living at home? Because frankly, darling, you've seemed quite miserable."

"I know, but it will get better," Esther answered. She felt like a stubborn six-year-old, arms folded, expression mutinous.

"Will it? Things don't magically get better, my darling. Just as I won't magically be happy in China. It takes work. Commitment. Happiness is a choice, not a mood that just comes on you when everything is aligned just right, the waters of life still and peaceful."

Esther had nothing to say to that. She wished she could just sneak away upstairs, but she knew her mother wouldn't let her.

"Esther, look, let me be honest here." Uh-oh. She was definitely in trouble now. "After Jamie died, I felt low. Really low." Esther looked up in shock. She hadn't been expecting that. "I ended up seeing a therapist, to talk through the grief, but also other things that came up. When something big happens, something bad, it can make you start to question everything. Wonder. Doubt... even the biggest and most important things. Especially those."

"Mum..."

"No, listen." Ruth held up a hand as she gave Esther a stern look. "I understand that you weren't happy with Will, and there are probably a lot of reasons for that. But you can't walk away from seven years of marriage without trying. It's not fair to Will or to you, and it's not right. And the truth is, I thought I raised you better than that."

"Mum!" Esther jerked back as if she'd been slapped, shocked at how hurt she felt.

"Well, I did," Ruth said calmly. "I understand needing to come back here and hide away for a while. I understand needing a change, giving up your job, all that. But Will is a good man, and as far as I know there hasn't been any infidelity or abuse, has there?"

"No," Esther muttered, blushing. "Of course there hasn't been anything like that."

"Well, then." Ruth placed both hands flat on the table, as if coming to a decision. "I think you need to try again with Will. I'll say it as plain as that. I'll also say you need to sort yourself out first, and that might mean some counselling, talking to a therapist like I did. There's no shame in it, Esther."

"I know," Esther mumbled, but she thought she'd rather have her gall bladder removed with a pair of tweezers. She didn't like to talk about her feelings, and neither did Will, which was why they were where they currently were.

"I love you," Ruth said, a catch coming into her voice. "That's why I'm saying all this. You know that, don't you?"

"Yes," Esther said, her voice catching as well. She believed her mother completely. "I know, Mum. I love you, too."

Chapter Eleven

ESTHER STOOD ON the threshold of The Queen's Sorrow, her heart thudding uncomfortably as she perused the crowded pub. She was due to meet Mark Taylor there, as much as she didn't really want to. After her rather reckless acceptance of his invitation at the coffee morning, she realized she didn't have his mobile number to cancel, and she'd been reluctant to send the message through Rachel.

For the last few days, her mother's surprisingly stern words had been ringing in Esther's ears, and making her chest hurt. *I thought I'd raised you better than that.* She'd bristled at her mother's tone, but inside she'd cringed because Ruth was right. Esther hadn't treated Will fairly, but she also didn't know if she could have done otherwise. She'd been in such a wretched place, and crawling out of the darkness felt like the hardest thing she'd done, and she'd barely started.

Still, having a drink with a single, attractive man on the heels of all that hardly felt like the right or wisest course of action. Yet here she was.

"Esther!" Mark called to her, waving from a cosy table at the back. Esther plastered a smile on her face and immediately felt it slip. She really didn't want to be here.

"Let me get you a drink," Mark said, rising as she approached the table. "What would you like?"

"A glass of white wine, please, but I'll pay—"

"Nonsense." She gave him what she hoped was a quelling look, but it seemed to bounce off him. "You can get the next round."

The trouble was, she didn't want there to be a next round. Feeling miserable, Esther sank onto a stool and watched Mark weave his way through the crowd towards the pub. The Queen's Sorrow was the village's posh pub, with an open fireplace and squashy chairs, and an air of relaxed, restrained cheer that was a far cry from the raucous feeling at The Bell. Not that Esther had ever been in The Bell, but she'd walked outside it on a weekend evening, heard the shouts, jeers, and catcalls.

She let her gaze sweep over the crowd, grateful that for once she didn't recognize anyone. The last thing she wanted was it getting back to Will that she'd been out having a drink with a man. Of course, just because she didn't recognize anyone, didn't mean they didn't recognize her. That was the joy and headache of living in Thornthwaite and being the vicar's daughter. Someone here was bound to recognize her, just as the news was bound to get back to Will. She couldn't avoid it.

"Here we are." Mark placed a glass of white wine down in front of her with a flourish, and placed a glass of red in front of his seat. Will never drank wine. Somehow, seeing that glass of red, made Esther miss him more.

"I'm not sure I should have come out tonight," she blurted as Mark settled himself across from her.

He frowned and took a sip of wine. "Why not?"

"Because... because I've separated from my husband but it's still very new. And I'm not sure I'm ready for... well, anything." Esther took a gulp of wine, needing the crisp, tangy comfort of it.

"But we're just friends," Mark said in an oh-so reasonable tone. "Having a drink. Surely your husband wouldn't object to that, even if you were still together?"

He would, Esther knew. Just as she would. She and Will had only needed each other. The thought of Will going out for a drink with some woman made her want to laugh with sheer disbelief, or possibly sway with terror. She definitely wasn't ready for this.

"I'm sorry," she said.

"No, I'm sorry." Mark smiled wryly, raking a hand through his hair. "Clearly I rushed things. Look, finish your wine, we can chat while you do it, and then you're free to go. Hopefully my company won't be too burdensome for a few minutes."

"It's not that it's burdensome—"

"I know, I know, I was just joking." His smile deepened.

"Why did you get separated, if you don't mind me asking? Is that too personal a question?"

Yes, it most certainly was. Mark must have seen that in her face for he had the grace to blush and duck his head. "Sorry, obviously it is. What shall we talk about, then? What do you do for work?"

"I was working for Natural England but I've just taken a redundancy package." At least, she'd composed the email and had it in her drafts folder. She wasn't quite ready to press send, but she might do it on Monday.

"Redundancy, eh?" Mark looked impressed. "Now that sounds like a sweet deal, getting a fat wodge of dosh to walk away from work."

"Well… yes, I suppose." Although she wouldn't put it quite like that.

"So, what are you going to do? I know you're behind that community garden scheme…"

"Yes, that's my plan. After that, who knows?" Roger had brought the signup sheet home from the coffee morning and Esther had been heartened to see twenty signatures on it.

She'd looked into applying for a council grant, and had even tentatively booked the village hall for a community meeting next week. All she had to do was put up posters in the village and of course think about what on earth she was going to say.

But she was starting to feel excited, like a flower unfurling inside her after a long, hard winter, and that was a good feeling. Mostly.

Mark asked her a bit about the community garden, and she asked him about his job teaching music, travelling around local schools to offers lessons in violin and piano. He seemed like a nice-enough bloke, and in a different life she might have felt a little catch of interest. As it was, as soon as her wine was finished, she was glad to make her escape, and Mark noticed with a wry grimace.

"So do you think we'll do this again?"

"Probably not," Esther admitted honestly. "But who knows?"

"Look me up when you think you're ready to move on, then."

"I will," Esther promised, but she doubted she would.

She walked out into the fresh, cool night, the sky clear and full of stars, breathing a loud sigh of relief. So dating was definitely not on her horizon, but was she actually trying to reconcile with Will?

The possibility sent her stomach writhing as if a pit of snakes had just taken residence there. She remembered the look of cold contempt on his face, and cringed. Would he really be interested in anything from her now, never mind what was on her heart? And did she even know how to go about baring that vital organ?

Esther started walking back to the vicarage, her mind still in a ferment. Yet as she turned down the darkened lane and walked past the church, something in her inexplicably lightened. She couldn't explain it, really, and yet she felt it; her heart buoyed just a little as she approached the square hulk of the vicarage and climbed up its weathered steps. She wasn't dreading coming home. Far from it.

"I'm home," she called, and heard both her parents' distant calls back. Roger emerged from his study, glasses pushed up onto his forehead, his hair askew.

"Hello, darling. Where have you been?"

"Out at the pub."

"With friends?" He seemed cheered by that idea, and Esther decided not to enlighten him further.

"Er, yes." She smiled and Roger wandered back into his study.

Esther found her mother upstairs, curled up on a sofa, reading one of the historical sagas she loved. The smile she gave Esther as she poked her head in the door was warm and genuine, and made Esther feel suddenly emotional.

"Hey, Mum."

"Is everything all right?"

"Everything's fine." Esther perched on the edge of the sofa. "I went for a drink at the pub."

"With…"

"A friend." Esther took a quick breath. "I've thought about what you said the other day, though. About needing to talk to Will."

Ruth's expression softened. "I'm sorry if I sounded harsh…"

"No, you didn't. You weren't. I haven't been fair to Will. I know that. It's just…" Another breath, this one feeling as if she had to drag it into her lungs. "I'm not sure I have the strength or the courage to talk to him, especially now that he probably hates me."

"He doesn't hate you, Esther."

"You don't know what I said to him."

"I know Will. I know the man is as steady and sure as a rock. He might be angry, he might be hurt, but he'll listen."

Esther nodded slowly. He would listen, but what would she say?

Two days later, on Monday evening, Esther stood in the parish hall, her heart thumping against her ribs as she shuffled papers in front of her. It was quarter to seven and no one was in the hall for the first meeting of the community garden scheme. Maybe no one would come, a possibility that filled Esther with both disappointment and a treacherous relief.

She'd spent the weekend papering the village with posters, helped by Rachel, who had been kicking around because Dan had a Saturday surgery.

"When do you two ever see each other?" Esther had asked as she Blu-tacked a poster to the front window of the village's post office shop.

Rachel had shrugged. "We manage."

Esther glanced at her sister curiously, noting the deliberately bland expression.

"Shall we put them up in both pubs?" Rachel suggested, the wind tangling her dark hair around her face. "And what about on the noticeboard up by the new estate, and in front of the primary school?"

"Yes and yes," Esther answered. She decided not to ask any more about Dan. She didn't particularly like people prying into her business, and so she wouldn't do it to anyone else.

Despite all the posters they'd put up, as well as the twenty signatures on the coffee morning sheet, Esther had serious doubts as to whether anyone would turn up. It was now ten to seven and the platter of cupcakes she'd bought from Morrisons was looking decidedly forlorn, as well as luridly coloured. She glanced down at the remarks she'd written down, bullet points that seemed laughable in an empty room. *Welcome everyone and thank them for coming.* Right.

Her mind, as it usually did during these moments, cast back to Will. She'd been trying to work up the courage to see him, talk to him, but it would already be four weeks since their separation on Wednesday—nearly an entire month. It had gone by horribly slowly, at least at first, although since she'd been able to focus on the garden idea the days had sped up faster. The nights were long, though, and really, what was she measuring? Was life simply something to be got through?

The protesting creak of the front door had Esther looking up in surprise. A woman about her own age with a head of curly blond hair and wind-reddened cheeks was coming in, unwinding a long, multi-coloured scarf from around her neck. It might be early April now, but it was still nippy at night, and would be all the way through the summer.

"Hi," Esther blurted, feeling unaccountably nervous. She didn't do nervous, at least she hadn't used to, but now she felt as if everything gave her a wobbly. She tried to smile. "Are you here for the community garden meeting?" Just her luck if the woman thought she was walking into a Zumba class.

"Yes, I am. You're leading it, aren't you? Esther?"

"Yes..."

"I'm Sophie West." She held out a hand which Esther shook.

"Nice to meet you."

"I think I was the year below you in school," Sophie answered with a little laugh. "But you probably don't remember me."

"Oh, well..." Esther wracked her memory but primary school felt like a lifetime ago.

"Never mind. You never know the children in the year below you, do you? You're always looking up."

"Yes, I suppose..." Small talk had never been her forte, and they were both made aware of it now. Still Esther tried, because what else could she do? It looked like it was going to be her and Sophie for the evening. "So you've lived in the village a long time?"

"I went away for a while. First to uni, then to London to

make my fortune." She grimaced good-naturedly. "It didn't happen, but I met my husband and we moved back here when we had kids—I've got two—and he managed to land a job working for the council. What about you? You're married, I think…?" She wrinkled her nose, waiting for Esther to trot out the potted version of her history.

"Um, yes. I am… married." That came out in jerks that no doubt made Sophie wonder about the state of her marital bliss.

"Kids…?"

"Nope." She'd meant to sound light but somehow she made even 'nope' sound terse and unfriendly. Esther looked down at her papers again and gave them a needless shuffle. "Will anyone else come, do you reckon? Have a cupcake."

"Thanks, I will." While Sophie helped herself to a cupcake iced in bright green, Esther willed another person to come through the door.

And then someone did—an old codger from coffee morning, and then another young woman who knew Sophie and soon they were nattering away about something at the school, and then a couple more from the coffee morning, and then an urbane-looking man in his fifties who was almost certainly a weekender, and soon the hall was filling up.

Esther felt both thrilled and terrified. The cupcakes were going and the hall was filled with exuberant chatter, and just as she was about to attempt to call the meeting to order, Will walked through the door.

The sight of him literally turned her breathless. She felt it catch in her chest and she froze to the spot, her gaze sweeping over him, remembering him even as she searched for changes. It had only been a week since she'd last seen him, but it felt like a lifetime.

He looked the same, and that was a relief. His hair was ruffled and messy, his face wind-reddened and weather-beaten, his eyes as bright a blue as ever—and they fastened on her as she gazed at him avidly and Esther felt something inside her clang. Hard.

The look went on for another taut few seconds, and she couldn't tell a thing from the look on Will's inscrutable face. He was poker-faced most of the time, but over seven years of marriage she'd learn to decipher the faintest twitch of an eyebrow or quirk of a lip. Now she couldn't tell anything. It was if the map of their shared life had already faded, so the shared landmarks were no longer recognizable.

Will looked away, and people started taking their seats, the chatter dying down even though Esther hadn't said anything. Almost as if on cue they all fell silent and turned to her, waiting for her to speak.

"Er…" Not the best start. She looked at the crowd of expectant faces, all, or at least most, of them friendly, and swallowed. Why was she so nervous? What had happened to her brisk take-charge attitude?

Then, out of the corner of her eye, she saw Will and he

gave her the faintest quirk of his mouth—so small perhaps he didn't even realize—and yet it heartened her. It was as good as a smile, or even a big, cheesy grin. She took a breath and started talking.

Later, when people were milling around, gathering coats, chatting, and scoffing the last few cupcakes, Esther saw Will slip out before she could speak to him, and her heart, which had been buoyed by the meeting's success, started to plummet. She didn't even know what she wanted—Will to sweep her up in his arms? It would be so unlike him she almost wanted to laugh. And yet she still wished he hadn't gone. Maybe she would have worked up the courage to talk to him, even ask him to talk properly, whatever that meant.

"So, when do you think we'll be able to organize the work party?" Sophie, the woman who had entered first, looked at her with an expectant smile.

"Why not this weekend?" Esther suggested, resolutely turning her gaze from the door of the hall which had just banged shut. "The sooner we get going, the better, and I'm away in Manchester the weekend after. It is April, after all." Although the amount of organization to get things sorted for this weekend was staggering. She'd have to rent a tiller, and organize coffee and sandwiches, and maybe a rota. All of it felt daunting, yet also invigorating.

Soon everyone was trickling away, and Esther turned off the lights and space heaters and locked the door to the hall, to return to the post office shop the next morning. Such was village life.

She was starting to walk back to the vicarage, the night dark and starless all around as clouds shifted across the moon, when a shadow peeled itself off the wall and fell in step beside her.

"Hello, Esther."

"Will." She came to a shocked halt, blinking in the dark to try to make out his face, and more importantly, his expression. "I didn't expect you to come."

"I know." Somehow that hurt, although she knew it shouldn't. Her mind felt emptied out, her tongue thick in her mouth. She couldn't think of a thing to say. "Seems like a good idea, anyway," Will said. "This garden thing."

"It was my father's idea."

He nodded, and the conversation petered out. Why couldn't she say something important and real? *Because you never do.* Frustrated with herself, Esther stared at him mutely. She really was no good at this.

"I'm glad you came," she blurted, shifting where she stood as she fidgeted with the strap of her bag. "I mean, it was good of you. Kind. Considering..." She trailed away, and still Will didn't speak.

"Considering," he repeated after what felt like an endless moment. "Considering what?"

He certainly wasn't making this easy for her, but then, why should he? "Look, Will," Esther said, her tone coming out too loud, too strident. "I'm no good at this. What I'm trying to say is…" She took a deep breath. What was she trying to say? "I was hoping we could maybe, you know, talk."

Will stared. And stared. "Talk," he finally repeated, once again his tone terribly neutral, giving nothing away. Giving nothing good away, anyway, and Esther would have appreciate being thrown a bone.

"Yes, talk."

"About?"

Jeez. Esther took another deep breath. Soon she'd be hyperventilating. "Well, I mean, I just feel that we could maybe, you know, one day find something to…" She was officially babbling, and about nothing. This was so *hard*. She and Will didn't do this kind of thing. How did they start? And when they did talk, *if* they did talk, what on earth would she say? "I don't know," she finished miserably.

Will let out a long, low rush of breath as he nodded slowly. "Well," he said. "You know where I am."

She nodded, still miserable. "Right."

Will nodded again and started walking down the street. Well, that had gone swimmingly. Not. Yet, considering everything, considering them, she couldn't have really expected anything else.

WILL DROVE HOME with his hands clenched on the steering

wheel and his jaw clenched tight. He was angry, and he didn't even know why. Esther wanted to talk. That was something. But she'd looked miserable, and Will was getting tired of feeling like a whipped dog cringing for another kick. He was tiring of all this feeling, full stop. He wanted things back the way they were, except the trouble was, that clearly hadn't worked. So what did? How could he and Esther move on, together? Especially when she was, as he'd learned yesterday when he'd stopped by the post office, going out for drinks with another man?

That had felt like a punch to the gut, leaving him winded. He'd given the man in the post office a flat stare and said nothing, but he'd felt like punching a wall. He was angry, and he didn't do angry. Not anymore. Not since David. But Esther's unhappiness had brought back the feelings that his brother's rebellion had—the hopeless churning, the despair that he just couldn't get it right, and so he ended up feeling frozen, acting numb, because he didn't know what else to do.

He wanted to go back to the beginning, start over somehow, but after seven years how did he manage that?

The idea that had been dancing around the fringes of his mind, an idea he really didn't like, was that maybe they just couldn't. Maybe they didn't work anymore, even after ten years together. Maybe they both had to move on. It was a horrible thought.

Will opened the door to the farmhouse, surprised that Toby didn't come whining for his dinner. It was later than usual, and he'd forgotten to feed him before he'd left for the community garden meeting, so he'd expected his dog to be waiting eagerly by the door.

"Tobes?" he called, unthinkingly using the nickname Esther had given the dog when he was little more than a pup. Toby whined, and Will heard the familiar brush of his tail against the stone-flagged floor.

"Oh, Tobes," he said, his heart twisting when he saw his dog, his faithful companion for eleven years, lying curled up next to the Aga, looking wretched. He crouched down and stroked his head, noting the way Toby barely moved.

He'd seen enough animals in pain over the years to know what was happening. His dog was old and arthritic and definitely slowing down; he'd known that, but he hadn't realized how tired Toby had become. There had been signs, Will realized, over the last few days; Toby had left his food, and he hadn't wanted to go outside. Will had noticed, but he'd been too full of other thoughts to make much of it. Now he saw the truth plainly, and it just about felled him. His dog was dying.

Toby lay his head on his paws and whined again.

"I'm sorry, bud," Will whispered. After all his big talk about how Esther could find him if she wanted, he'd have to call her. She needed to know about Toby. Right then it felt like one more loss on top of too many already. Will wasn't sure he had it in him to take much more.

Chapter Twelve

ESTHER'S MOBILE RANG just as she stepped into the vicarage's porch, and her heart turned over when she saw it was Will. Had he changed his mind…

"Will?"

"Esther, it's Toby." His voice was brusque and Esther's heart lurched.

"Toby…"

"He's an old boy, you know, and I came home tonight and he didn't get up."

Esther felt a strange panicky feeling sweep through her. "Maybe he's tired."

"No, Esther," Will said gently. "That's not it. I'm sorry, but I know a dying animal when I see one."

Esther let out a small, soft cry, panic replaced by pain. Not Toby. Not their sweet, gentle dog, not on top of everything else. "No…"

"Why don't you come over?" Will said gruffly. "He'll want to see you."

Esther's chest was so tight it hurt to breathe. "Can't you

take him to the vet… Dan…"

"It's too late for that. Trust me, I know."

It hurt to speak, to breathe. "Okay," she managed after a moment. "I'll come over now." She grabbed her car keys and went right back out, without even telling her parents where she was. They'd worry, but she couldn't take their concern, not now. Not when, after all this time, she was so very close to completely falling apart, the final turn of the screws and loosening of the bolts.

The drive through the dark felt cold and lonely, the fields on either side of the narrow track falling away to blackness. When she pulled into the farmyard, the lights of the long, low farmhouse winking in the darkness, she felt a pang of both longing and relief. She was home.

Inside, the kitchen was lit only by a lamp by the old, fraying armchair by the fireplace, and Will was sat down by the Aga, Toby's dear old greying head in his lap. Esther let out a choking sound of grief.

"How did this happen?" she gasped out as she came towards them.

"He's old," Will said gently as he stroked Toby's head, "and he has been slowing down a lot, sleeping more and more. He hasn't gone up the stairs for years."

"But I thought that was just arthritis."

"It's all part of it, isn't it?" He gave her a tired, sad smile. "For the last few days he's been off his food, not wanting to go out. I should have realized… but this is natural, Esther. A natural part of life."

But it didn't feel natural. Esther shed her jacket and bag and then sat on the other side of Toby, running a hand along his back. "Is he... is he in pain?" she asked, a catch in her voice.

"He doesn't seem to be too bad. If he seems like he's still struggling in the morning, I'll take him to Dan."

"You mean to..."

"Yes." Despite the incredible sadness of the scene, there was something strangely and wonderfully steady and reassuring about Will in this moment. He was a rock to lean on, a comforting presence in a way he hadn't been during her miscarriage. Maybe because she hadn't let him.

It was too much to think of now, to wonder and regret. Esther scooted closer to Toby and stroked his head, his fur silky under her fingers. "Poor old Toby," she whispered. "He was only a year old when we started dating—do you remember?"

"I remember."

Esther gazed down at the dog, the pressure in her chest growing tighter, making it harder and harder to breathe. "The first time I came over for dinner..." she began, and then had to stop.

"He climbed up on my chair and ate most of the pot of bolognaise sauce."

"And was horribly sick afterwards, poor thing."

"I thought you'd never come back."

His words were a thrum in his chest, an ache of poignancy in his voice.

"It takes more than a mischievous puppy to scare me off," Esther said, and then fell silent. They were skating dangerously close to the thin ice of their relationship, the black waters of untried emotion swirling all around them.

"What does scare you off then?" Will asked quietly.

Esther kept her gaze on Toby as she continued to stroke his head. The kitchen was quiet and dim, warm and cosy. It even smelled familiar—like coal fires and wet wool, a hint of coffee and well-worn leather. The smell of home, of Will. "I scared myself off," she whispered. "I'm sorry, Will. I'm sorry I didn't... I couldn't..." She wasn't going to be able to say anymore. The tears that she'd been suppressing for so long—years, decades—were finally going to fall, and Esther feared there was nothing she could do about it.

Losing Toby on top of everything else was going to be too much. She'd been trying to move on, to get a start on a new life, but it all felt like so much pointless, ceaseless striving now. She hadn't moved on. She wasn't any better. She was still hurting inside, still wretched and guilty, and worse, she was now crying. Quite a lot.

The first sob came out sounding like a burp, a little bubble of sound that she tried to suppress as she clapped her hand over her mouth. It was no good. Another sob escaped her, and then another, and then tears were streaming from her eyes and her shoulders were shaking and she felt as if she were falling apart. Literally falling apart right there on the kitchen floor, bits and pieces breaking off until there would be nothing left.

"Esther." Will leaned across Toby and put a heavy hand on his shoulder. *"Esther."*

She couldn't see him through the haze of her tears, but she felt his strong arms come around her, and somehow he'd managed to draw her gently around Toby and onto his lap, as if she were a child, or perhaps a treasure. She leaned her head against his shoulder as he stroked her hair and she cried like she never had before.

It felt both good and painful and somewhat humiliating to let it all out; it was as if a dam had broken inside her and everything, absolutely everything, came rushing at him. Her shoulders shook, her eyes streamed, and the sounds coming out of her mouth were... well, they were making *her* cringe, because they sounded so guttural and awful. She was full on ugly crying, and that was so not her.

And yet somehow it was—the new her, the broken her, the real her, underneath the old gloss of know-it-all capability that had definitely lost its shine. Will held her and stroked her hair, silent as ever, and so nice as it was to be held Esther had no idea what he was feeling. Maybe he was appalled. *She* was appalled. She was snivelly and snotty and hiccuping. Not a good look at the best of times, and as for now...

"I'm sorry," she managed after what could have been an

hour but was hopefully only a few minutes.

"Don't be sorry."

"I don't cry, though."

"Seems like you needed to."

She glanced down at Toby, whose eyes fluttered closed. "Is he—" she began, sounding panicked, and Will's arms tightened around her.

"He's just sleeping, Esther. You'll know when."

She was silent for a moment, breathing in the quiet and the fragile sense of peace, feeling as if she were in the eye of a storm. "I've never seen someone—any creature—die." She should have, living on a farm, working as she did, but death had always been kept behind closed doors, in barns or sheds or dark, quiet corners. At a distance, even when it had been important.

"It's a natural process," Will said after a moment, one big hand cradling her head like she was a newborn baby he was palming. "But it doesn't feel natural, not ever, and sometimes it feels long and like, well, hard work."

"And sometimes not." The words slipped out, before she even knew she was saying them. "Sometimes it happens so quick, you don't even know…" Surely she couldn't be crying again. She didn't have any tears left. And as she drew a quick breath, Esther realized she wasn't crying. The pain went too deep for that, pain she'd pushed down and held back for far too long. For twenty years.

"Jamie," Will said softly, and Esther didn't answer because she couldn't, and also because she didn't need to.

"It's always hard," Will said quietly.

"Your parents, I know…" He'd lost his parents in a car accident when he was nineteen, years before Esther had ever met him. They'd been coming home from a shopping trip in Keswick, and had been hit by a lorry taking a short-cut on a single-track road. A matter of seconds, both of them killed instantly. Just like Jamie.

Had that brought them together, way back when? They'd shared their stories on the second date, quietly, without fuss. And they hadn't talked about it again, not really, but it had been there, the common knowledge, the shared grief, a burden borne by two, not one. Which, Esther realized now, was important in its own way. Why hadn't she realized how important that was? Why hadn't she shared her grief, even the awfulness of her relief, over the miscarriage with Will?

She took a deep breath and then a big sniff. The tears were still there, trembling under her lids, in her chest. "I didn't see Jamie die," she whispered, half-amazed she was talking about this at all. "I wasn't there." Will was silent, waiting, and somehow that made Esther brave saying more. "I was in class—first lesson, maths. Someone came and got me, told me to go to the head teacher's office. I thought I was in trouble, and that was what worried me. Not that something might have happened." She twisted around to gaze up at him, his face barely visible in the shadowy room.

"Why didn't that occur to me? Why was I only thinking about myself?"

"It was a natural thought, Esther."

"Was it?" She shook her head, surprised by the strength of the pain and regret she still felt. She'd buried it for so long, papered over the cracks till she was nothing but spackle and paste. No wonder she was crumbling apart. Amazing, really, that it hadn't happened sooner.

"Of course it was. Thinking the worst—why should you? Why should you beat yourself up for not doing it?"

"I know..." she said, because when he said it like that it seemed so obvious and sensible. The trouble was, it didn't *feel* obvious and sensible.

"Let me ask you this," Will said in a low voice, after a few moments had gone by. "Did... did your experience with Jamie, your grief, the fact that you couldn't do anything about it... is that... did that..." He stopped, and Esther twisted around again to look at him. His forehead was furrowed in concentration, a shadow of grim uncertainty in his eyes. Whatever he was trying to say, it was hard for him.

But then all of this was hard. They never talked like this, not ever. And as for Toby... Esther's heart spasmed as she glanced down at the dog she'd loved for ten years. He looked so sad, his eyes droopy, his breathing laboured. Poor, lovable beast. She bent to stroke his head once more.

"Good dog," she whispered. "Good boy."

"Esther." Will sounded more strident now, almost stroppy. "Tell me this." She stilled, her hand resting on Toby's silky head. "Did your not wanting to have a baby... did it have anything to do with your brother?"

"What?" She felt jolted, as if she'd missed the last step in a staircase. His question seemed absurd, connecting dots that were miles apart. "Of course not," she said automatically, but already a terrible unease was growing inside her, a cancer of doubt taking her over. "Why did you ask that?" she asked abruptly. "What made you think of it?"

"I don't know," Will admitted. "I'm not good with stuff like this, you know that. But it just seems... it just doesn't make sense. Something doesn't anyway, and I don't think it's just me being thick. At least I hope it's not." He put his hands on her shoulders and turned her to face him. "What are you afraid of?"

The question was so blunt, so stark, that Esther answered before she'd even framed the words in her head. "I'm afraid of getting it wrong."

"Getting what wrong?"

"Motherhood. Babies. Life." She drew a quick, shuddery breath. "It's so important, and I might mess it up."

"Why do you think you would?"

"Because... because..." She searched fruitlessly for an answer that made sense. "I don't know," she admitted. "I've always had a thing about control, I suppose. About working hard and getting it right."

Will frowned. "Always?"

"As long as I can remember. And I suppose…" She paused, thinking through things, feeling her way slowly. "I suppose it got worse after Jamie. Because that was so out of my control. I wasn't even there. Maybe if I was…"

"Esther, you can't think that way. There's no point, trust me."

"Well." Another quick breath. She wasn't sure how much more she could take of this intensity. "I know that. But it's hard not to feel it all the same." She shifted herself off Will's lap, suddenly conscious of how ridiculous it all seemed. He'd been cradling her as if she were a baby, or one of his precious lambs.

She kept her face averted as she repositioned herself on the other side of Toby and gazed down at his dear face, his greying muzzle. "Do you remember," she asked quietly, "how he always used to stand by the door and nudge it with his nose as soon as you put your boots on?"

"Yeah." Will smiled faintly. "He hasn't done that for a while."

"No, he hasn't," Esther acknowledged with a jolt of painful realization. "You're right, he hasn't climbed the stairs in ages, either—years, I think. How has he got old without me realizing?"

"That's how life happens."

Esther had a prickling feeling that Will wasn't just talking about their dog. How had they come to this place of strangeness, of not really knowing or understanding each other, after so many years? Had they slipped into the well-worn grooves of married life, not realizing those grooves were getting farther and farther apart? Or had they never really known each other, not in the way that mattered? Esther didn't know which possibility was more depressing.

The hours slipped past silently, both of them lost in their own thoughts, as Toby's breathing became more and more laboured, his eyes closed. As Esther watched, he seemed to be losing some essential part of himself; he hadn't really changed, and yet he was diminished.

Sometime after midnight, in the darkest part of the night, he slipped away. Esther felt a leaden sadness; she'd already shed her tears. But it still brought a lump to her throat when Will stooped to pick up Toby and cradled his limp body to his chest.

"I'll take him outside," he said quietly. "I'll bury him in the afternoon, when the ground has warmed up."

Esther nodded, the tears she'd thought she'd already shed starting to swim to the surface. She stood up, her muscles aching from sitting on the floor so long, and watched as Will quietly left the house.

Will had to miss Toby even more than she did. He'd got him as a puppy before they'd started dating, had had him by his side in the sheep fields day after mucky day. A man's best friend, indeed.

The kitchen felt lonely and silent with Will and Toby gone. Esther halfheartedly reached for her coat, her hand falling to her side before she'd grabbed it. The thought of heading back to the vicarage now made her feel even more drained than she already was. She sent a text to her parents, just in case they'd noticed she hadn't come home.

"There, now." Will came into the kitchen, closing the door behind him with a heavy thud. "It's freezing out there tonight."

"Is it?" It wasn't unheard of to snow this time of year, especially on higher ground. "I suppose I should go…"

"Don't." Esther blinked at him in surprise, and Will stumbled to explain. "I just mean, it's late, it's been a long, hard night. We have a spare room."

It was only a little over a mile back to Thornthwaite, and yet right then it felt like a very long mile. And the truth was, Esther didn't want to go. She didn't want to be alone. And yet…

"Please," Will said quietly, and somehow that sold it.

She nodded, and Will turned to fill up the kettle and switch it on. It wasn't until he'd reached for the fleece-lined bottles that she realized what he was doing, and it almost made her cry all over again.

They worked in sweet, silent harmony, filling the hot-water bottles, locking doors and turning off lights. Esther almost whistled for Toby, only to remember afresh and she drew in a revealingly hitched breath instead.

"I know," Will said, and she knew he did.

They went up the narrow, creaky stairs to the upstairs

hallway, everything cluttered and shabby and achingly familiar.

"I'll get sheets…" Will began, and Esther put her hand on his arm.

"Don't," she said simply. She really didn't want to be alone. Will turned to her in surprise. "I just want…" she began haltingly, embarrassed to explain, and he nodded.

"I know, Esther. I know."

And once again, he did. They undressed in silence, Esther stripping down to her thermals, and got into the bed together, bodies bumping softly in the dark. Will's arms came around her and he drew her against him, her back against his chest as she cradled the hot-water bottle against her stomach and for the first time in what felt like a million years, Esther relaxed. And then she slept.

Chapter Thirteen

WHEN ESTHER WOKE to bright morning sunlight, she knew Will must have been up for hours. His side of the bed was cold and empty, and as she lay there, huddled under the heavy duvet, staring up at the ceiling, she remembered how she'd slept in his arms all night and didn't know how to feel about that. Didn't know how to feel about anything.

She remembered too how she'd cried in his arms and all the things she'd said, and inwardly she cringed and squirmed. She didn't like it. She didn't like it at all, Will knowing that, listening to her whinge and blubber. But, on some level, she knew that was what marriage was meant to be, what intimacy was... and if it had been missing from hers and Will's relationship, well, that wasn't a good thing, was it? She'd felt its lack, and yet she still felt cringy and uncertain now.

She got out of bed and took a shower in the old Victorian tub with its trickle of water, using the shampoo and soap and even the razor that were all hers, left where she'd last put them down. It felt odd, somehow, to think of Will living and moving about her things, as if she'd just gone away for a week and was going to come back very soon.

And was she?

Amidst all the emotion and sadness of last night, they hadn't talked about that. They hadn't even come close. And Esther still felt jumbled-up inside, unsure what she wanted or was ready for. What she was capable of.

She got out of the shower, towelling herself off quickly in the frigid air, and then dressed in her clothes from last night, stealing a pair of Will's thick wool socks. Downstairs, in the morning light, the kitchen looked as messy and cluttered as ever, and with nothing else to do, Esther set about cleaning it.

She was just setting the last plate in the dish drainer— they'd never bothered with a dishwasher—when Will came into the kitchen, stamping the mud off his boots.

His bright blue gaze took in her presence by the sink, the clean dishes, the table cleared of piles of post and dirty dishes. As he closed the door, the kettle began to whistle.

"Oh." He sounded surprised, and cautiously pleased. "Thanks."

"I think this lot was worse than this place before we were married," Esther remarked. "Back then you used to do the dishes, as I recall, at least on occasion."

"It is lambing season," Will reminded her. "And back then I was trying to impress you."

Her stomach tumbled over. "And now you're not?"

Will shrugged, his eyes both serious and sad. "Is it worth trying?"

They were tiptoeing towards the heart of the matter, and Esther felt a self-preserving instinct to edge away. "I don't want or need you to impress me, Will. It's... it's never been about that."

She turned towards the kettle, needing to keep busy. "Cup of tea?"

"All right, then."

"And breakfast? Have you eaten?"

"Not yet."

It was easier to busy herself pouring coffee, frying eggs and bacon, than to look Will in the eye and have to talk about all this stuff.

It wasn't until they were sitting opposite each other at the old farmhouse table that Will spoke again, and what he said shocked Esther to her core.

"I think what we need to do," he said as he took a sip of coffee and set his mug down with a purposeful thunk, "is start dating again."

⫸⫷

ESTHER'S EYES WIDENED and her lips parted soundlessly. She was completely shocked, and no wonder. It wasn't the most obvious suggestion, and yet in the early hours of the morning, when he'd been tending to the animals, it had seemed right. Unfortunately now he felt fairly ridiculous for saying such a thing, and so he shovelled eggs into his mouth instead of explaining what he'd meant.

"Date again?" Esther repeated incredulously. "How are we supposed to do that?"

"The usual way, I suppose, although I'm not even sure there's any 'again' about it," Will replied with a swallow and a shrug. "Did we date much in the first place?"

"Will, we dated for two years." Esther still looked flummoxed.

"But it wasn't really dating, was it?" Will pressed. "It was… it was just life."

Something flickered in her eyes, although whether it was horror or interest Will couldn't say.

"What are you suggesting, then?" she asked. "That we get all sappy and romantic?" She sounded both amused and a bit revolted, and it made Will smile.

"I can't see us writing love notes and what not," he admitted. "But you said yourself something's been missing, and we both owe it to each other at least to give it a go, figuring out what that is."

Esther shook her head slowly, and Will's gut tightened. It hadn't been easy, coming up with this suggestion. It hadn't been easy, holding Esther while she cried or in his arms all night. He'd been filled with both longing and doubt, and a terrible, terrifying uncertainty. He didn't know what she needed, and he really didn't know if he was the one who could give it to her.

But he wanted to try.

"It would feel silly," she said. "Going on dates when we've been married for eight years."

"Then let's be silly."

Esther's head was lowered, her gaze on her barely-touched breakfast. "Do you still want to date me," she asked in a voice so quiet Will strained to hear, "after everything?"

"It seems I do." What else was he supposed to say? Yes, he was hurt, and, no, he didn't like her walking out on him, or telling him she didn't want his baby, and if she didn't want kids ever, he wasn't sure how he felt about that.

There were plenty of bumps on this particular road, but he still wanted to go down it. This was his marriage, after all. And he knew what it felt like to give up too soon, to walk away because he was angry and it seemed easier. He knew what it felt like, and it wasn't good. It was the worst thing in the world. He wasn't going to make the mistake he'd made with David, with Esther. Not if he could help it.

Esther was still silent, still not looking at him, and so Will kept eating. What else could he do? He felt as if he were wound too tightly instead, grief and fear and doubt all battling for place.

"So what would we do?" Esther asked finally. "Just go out to dinner at The Winter Hare? What?"

This was so not his strong suit. Will had no idea what

they'd do. In fact, right now, he had no idea what the heck he'd been thinking, suggesting they date. What did that even mean? In the early morning, as he'd cradled a new lamb, it had somehow made sense. They needed to go back to the beginning, to start over and treat each other as new people. That had felt right, at five a.m. Not so much now. "Something like that, I guess," he hedged. What else could he say? "A chance to get to know each other again." Which sounded like something he'd seen on a sappy greeting card. What was *wrong* with him? No wonder Esther was looking so unimpressed.

"All right," she said after an endless moment. "I guess we could try it." Which left Will feeling both exultant and extremely apprehensive. But at least they'd got somewhere, even if he didn't know where exactly that was.

>>>><<<<

BY THE TIME Esther climbed out of her car in front of the vicarage, she was feeling the effects of very little sleep. Her eyes were itchy and she felt as if she were viewing the world through a hazy veil, which was why she didn't even think before replying to her mother's apprehensive, "Where *were* you?" with "At Will's."

"At Will's?" Ruth's concern immediately transformed into cautious delight. "All night?"

"Yes—Toby died." The memory was like a heavy fist

ploughing into her stomach. "He was old, I know, but…"

"Oh, Esther. Darling. I'm so sorry." Ruth enveloped her in a warm, floury hug, and Esther breathed in the sugary-sweet scent of her mother, grateful for the comfort and the contact.

"Thanks, Mum."

"That's so hard."

"You know as well as anyone." Before Charlie, there had been first Max and then Molly, the black labs of her child-hood. Each one had been a friend.

"Yes." Ruth eased back and smiled at Charlie, who had not moved a muscle from his well-worn position by the Aga. "You try to prepare yourself, but it always comes as a shock."

"What will you do with Charlie, when you move to China?" The enormity of her parents' move hit her all over again, as it always did. "You can't take him, surely."

"No, and I don't think he'd want to go, even if we could. He's too old to change his ways, poor lad." She smiled again at Charlie, whose only sign of understanding any of the conversation was the twitch of his doggy eyebrows.

"So…?"

"I was hoping you and Will or Dan and Rachel might take him," Ruth admitted with a wry smile. "But I haven't asked anyone yet, obviously. I'm sure someone in the parish will take him, but I'm sure he'd rather be with family."

"What about Simon? So Charlie could stay here?"

"Yes, Simon too, of course." Ruth rubbed her forehead.

"For some reason I keep forgetting that Simon will be living here. It's so silly of me."

Except it wasn't silly at all, and Esther understood it perfectly. She couldn't imagine Simon living here. She couldn't imagine anyone other than her parents living here, filling up these rooms. But, despite her mother's wry smile, Esther could see a warning in her eyes not to push the subject, so she didn't. She was too tired anyway, and she had a lot of work to catch up on before she finished with Natural England next week, and then of course there was all the community garden stuff… She needed to arrange a work party for the next weekend, and send out emails, and rent a tiller or even two…

"You look shattered," Ruth remarked. "Maybe you should get some sleep."

It was ten o'clock in the morning and the day stretched ahead of her, seeming somewhat endless. "Maybe," Esther agreed, because she couldn't really imagine keeping her eyes open for another twelve hours. "What are you doing today, Mum?"

"Oh, I thought I'd sort through some things for the move," she said in a tone that, to Esther, sounded overly bright. "There's so much to do—I really should have started before now."

"Sort out some things? What kind of things?"

"Well, you know, furniture and such. We have far too much of it. Far too much of everything, really." Ruth turned away and began to wipe the top of the Aga's silver lids.

"Yes, but…" Along with Charlie, was everything to go? Why did the thought bother her so much? She felt like a little girl. "You're not going to give away everything, are you?"

"Not everything, no. Some of it Simon might want to keep. I don't think he has more than a sofa and a bed to his name. And I thought Rachel and Dan might want a few things, setting up home together, although who knows, perhaps our things are too shabby." Ruth let out a high laugh that subsided on a sigh. "Anyway, it certainly needs sorting out. We've just shoved things in boxes upstairs for the last thirty years. Most of it, I suspect, will go in the tip."

Which brought a lump to Esther's throat. "Do you want me to help?"

"I thought you were tired…"

She was, but this felt more important. She didn't want her mother to do this all alone. "I don't think I'll be able to sleep, actually. Let me make a pot of coffee and then I'll help. What are you going to tackle first?"

"I don't know if I have the stamina for the attics," Ruth admitted with a grimace. "Perhaps we could just go through the pantries."

"Is there much to go through in there?" Esther asked in surprise. Ruth just laughed and shook her head.

Twenty minutes later, armed with a large mug of coffee, Esther began to see why her mother had laughed. At first glance, the kitchen's two walk-in pantries had seemed like fairly innocuous propositions—everyday dishes, the fine china, food. Simple. Or not.

As Ruth went deeper into the pantry, out came the crystal serving dishes they'd picked up at a car boot sale and never used; the flower pots the children had sloppily painted over the years; the five-kilo bag of lentils Miriam had bought during a short-lived health kick. The pile of dusty, unused tat grew at both their feet, and despite the utter uselessness of much of it, Esther couldn't help but feel nostalgic.

"You really want me to keep that?" Ruth demanded with an arched eyebrow when Esther hesitated over a pair of silver-plated salt and pepper shakers in the shape of a pair of elephants. "They're completely impractical, we never used them, and they were a gift from someone whose name I've forgotten, who left the parish fifteen years ago. They were probably just getting rid of some of their old rubbish when they moved."

"I know you're right." Esther relegated the shakers to the pile. "It's just… it feels so… unsettling. Like you're pulling up anchor and suddenly we're all adrift." She pictured the house like a ship on the sea, bobbing amidst the foreign waves.

"I know this has been the only home you've really known," Ruth said, softening. "Sometimes it feels like the only home I've ever known."

"There's something weirdly reassuring about knowing all

this stuff is here," Esther tried to explain. "That you've never got rid of anything. That we can find whatever we need." That it hadn't changed.

"Somehow I don't think you're going to need ninety percent of what we kept, including all your GCSE textbooks and notes." Ruth rolled her eyes. "It was just that we had the space, so we kept it. But letting go of it all can be strangely liberating. At the end of the day, it's just stuff. You can't take it with you."

"Not to China, anyway," Esther quipped, and then braced herself when her mother gave her one of her serious looks.

"And not into eternity," she said quietly, and Esther resisted an eye roll. She felt badly, in a way, for not sharing her parents' faith, but there it was. She didn't.

Ruth sighed and reached for the next dusty item. It seemed Esther wasn't going to have to listen to a well-meaning lecture, after all.

By lunchtime they'd cleared out both pantries, and boxed up what could go to charity shops and taken the rest to the tip. Esther had offered to drive it all over, and it felt both sad and strangely liberating to toss the bags of rubbish into the skip.

Back at the vicarage, Ruth and Roger had both gone out and Esther realized she needed to make a start on preparations for the garden clear-out on Saturday. She brewed herself a cup of tea and then set about making lists and phone calls, arranging for a tiller to be delivered on the morning. She also spent a fair amount of time looking into getting not-for-profit status, and realized she could spend hours, if not days, snarled up in all the bureaucracy—making a charter, registering it, setting up accounts. But it would have to be done if this community garden was actually going to *be* something, and so she made notes and a few telephone calls about getting registered and also opening a bank account, and by evening she felt both invigorated and exhausted.

"You've been busy," Roger remarked as he came into the kitchen after having finished a pastoral meeting. "At least, you look as if you have."

"Busy but I'm not sure how productive," Esther answered as she gathered up sheets of paper with bits scribbled on them. "Research, mainly, but at least we'll be able to have a work day on Saturday."

"Have your mother bake for them," Roger advised. "Then they'll come out in droves."

"Dad…" Esther began impulsively, and then stopped. Roger turned to her, one eyebrow raised.

"Yes?"

"Do you… do you think Mum will bake in China?"

Roger cocked his head, his knowing gaze sweeping over Esther, making her feel like she had as a child, when she'd done something wrong and been called into his study. "Why do I think that's not really the question you care about?"

"I think you know what I mean."

"Yes, I think I do. What are you worried about, Esther? That your mother won't be happy in China?" As usual, her father nailed it square on the head, and so Esther decided to answer in kind.

"Yes," she said. "That's exactly what I'm worried about."

"Have you talked to her about it?"

"Yes."

"And what has she said?" Roger sounded remarkably unperturbed, so much so that Esther suspected he was quite certain of the answer.

"She said happiness was a choice—"

"Ah."

"But that still sounds rather bleak to me," Esther persisted. "Like you've got to work at it—"

"You have to work at just about anything worthwhile."

Esther was fast remembering she could not win a philosophical argument with her father. She'd tried, when she'd taken philosophy for an A level, but she'd been beaten before she'd barely managed a syllable.

"Don't you think anything in life should be easy?" she grumbled, and Roger shot a quick smile, full of humour and love.

"Yes, the decision to work at something. That's easy."

Esther rolled her eyes and Roger laughed. "Why don't you tell me about your plans for the garden while I attempt to make us a cup of tea?"

Esther smiled as her father filled the kettle. He liked to pretend he was utterly useless in the kitchen, but in fact he knew his way around fairly well. Esther remembered how he'd made a full fry-up every morning when Miriam had been born, and delivered breakfast in bed, complete with flowers and the newspaper, to her mother upstairs.

She was so lucky, she realized with a sudden pang. So, so lucky to have two parents who loved her absolutely—she'd never doubted that, not for a second—and were devoted to each other, as well. She'd had such a good model for marriage. Why did she seem to keep making missteps with her own?

Chapter Fourteen

T HE NEXT SATURDAY, the day of the community garden clearing, dawned sunny and warm, like a promise from Providence, although why Esther was thinking about Providence, she had no idea. Her parents must be slyly rubbing off on her.

Still, whatever the reason, she was grateful for the sunshine and warm breeze as she pushed the tiller back to the garden, wrangling it through the gate.

"Small is the gate and narrow the road that leads to life," Roger intoned, a sparkle in his eye, as he came up behind her and helped to shove it through.

"I'm not sure how much life there is in this garden yet," Esther quipped back. "It's looking pretty dead."

In fact, in the few weeks since she'd come at it with a pair of secateurs and a lot of determination, the brambles and nettles had started growing back, and everything looked wilder than ever. Her spirits, which had only just been beginning to lift, started to flag once more. How on earth was she really going to do this?

"So…" Roger planted his hands on his hips as he surveyed the scene. "What we need is coffee, tea, and plenty of flapjacks."

"That's not going to get this garden tilled," Esther said, feeling more hopeless by the second. What if no one came? What if people did come, and it was all too hard, too impossible?

"No, but it will get people motivated. Now help me set up a table."

"A table…"

A few minutes later they were dragging one of the old, weathered picnic tables from the garden to a space by the gate, and then Ruth came out bearing a tray of flapjacks, followed by several carafes of coffee and tea, and a platoon of mugs.

She'd just finished when people started arriving—first Sophie West, who smiled cheerfully and added a plate of homemade brownies to the table, and then surveyed the garden with interest, whistling under her breath.

"Wow, what a big space."

"And lots of weeds," Esther couldn't keep from adding, even though she knew she was just being gloomy.

"And lots of possibilities," Sophie answered. "How are we going to make a start?"

Good question. Esther wished she'd had more of a game plan. She was normally organized to the point of brutality, but somehow she'd lost that along with everything else.

"Only one person can manage the tiller," she said, thinking out loud, "but we'll need several people collecting the weeds, and someone coming behind raking out the soil…"

"That sounds about right," Sophie said. "Good thing there's quite a few of us."

In surprise, Esther turned and saw half a dozen people walking across the vicarage garden… including Will. She caught his eye and he gave one of his tiny quirks of a smile, and her heart turned over. She wondered if he still wanted to date her, and how on earth that was going to work. Maybe it had been a spur of the moment suggestion, after the intensity of their night together with Toby, one he now wished he hadn't made.

Toby… a pressure built in her chest and she took a deep breath to ease it. She needed to focus on the garden right now. On the future. Her future… whether it included Will or not.

The next half hour was a blur of activity as Esther organized everyone, Ruth poured coffee and handed out flapjacks, and Roger relaxed everyone with his easy bonhomie. Soon enough someone was behind the tiller, other people were cutting swathes through the wild, and yet others were gathering the waste into paper garden bags that they piled by the door.

The sun was warm and bright, the sky a deep blue, with fleecy clouds scudding across. It was the kind of spring day that only came once in a very blue moon to the usually wet and rainy lake district, and it lifted Esther's spirits even further, so she felt as if she were flying inside.

Several hours in, she could see the rich, black earth of the garden, and she began to envision how this blank canvas could become a beautiful picture.

They stopped for lunch after a couple of hours; most people had brought sandwiches and Ruth made more tea, and amazingly, brought out yet another plate of flapjacks. Her mother could magic baking anywhere, anytime, a gift Esther hoped she'd still be able to use... but she was coming to realize her mother's choices were not her business, and maybe there would be other gifts she could use. Other opportunities. Maybe life wasn't the single, straight road she kept trying to make it, but a meandering path with lots of bumps and surprises along the way, for everyone.

Now, perched on the crumbling foundation of a cold frame, sipping tea from a flask and tilting her face to the sun, Esther wanted to enjoy the twists and bumps, or at least take them in her stride... whatever they were.

"Hey there."

She turned to see Will standing next to her, squinting in the sunlight. "Hey."

He sat down next to her, one long, blue jean-clad leg stretched out in front of him. "It's going well."

"It is, isn't it?" Esther gazed around the half-ploughed stretch of earth. "It'll be quite a job removing all the rocks and roots and putting compost on, but still."

"It's a start, anyway, and people seem keen."

A round dozen of volunteers had showed up, besides her parents, Sophie, Will, Rachel and Dan, and Simon, and Esther had been both shocked and gratified by the number. "Yes, they do, actually."

"You sound surprised."

Esther gave a little, self-conscious laugh. "I suppose I am. This entire idea seemed mad, and it isn't as if I've made a success of much lately, is it?"

Will shook his head slowly. "Why do you say rubbish like that, Esther?"

"Rubbish?" She jerked back, affronted and a little hurt. "I thought I was just stating fact."

"It's as if you're always holding a scorecard," he continued. "Ticking things off or deleting points, grading yourself when there's no need."

She blinked, stung by his observation even as she recognized some truth in it. "Doesn't everyone do that, at least a little?"

Will shrugged. "Maybe, but it feels as if it's paralyzed you. Because for once in your life you didn't get the A star and now you don't know what to do."

Esther looked away, unable to answer as she tried to formulate her thoughts. "So what grade did I get?" she finally asked, only half joking, and Will shook his head.

"Seriously, Esther."

"I am being serious." Sort of.

"I know you are, that's the trouble." He sighed and stood up, holding a hand out to her. "I need to get back to the farm."

"Okay." Esther took his hand gingerly, feeling something like relief when his big hand closed over hers and he hauled her up. She'd always liked how strong Will was, how steady. She'd just never let herself depend on it.

"So, do you want to go out to dinner?"

"What?"

"I told you we should start dating." He stood there, as immovable as a rock, his gaze unblinking as he waited for her answer.

"I know you did, but… I thought maybe that was just…"

"A spur of the moment thing?" Will filled in. "Have I ever seemed like a spur of the moment bloke, Esther?"

"No." And she'd liked that, too. She'd always known where she was with Will. It was with herself that she didn't know where she was.

"So. Dinner."

"When?"

He shrugged. "You name the day."

Her heart and mind both raced. A date. Would it be hideously awkward, like they were play-acting at being a couple? She couldn't even imagine it. "I'm going to Manchester next weekend to try on bridesmaid dresses."

"Doesn't have to be a weekend."

"No..." Why was she hesitating? Either she wanted to do this or she didn't. And there was no real reason not to do it, except for her fear. And the lack of control. But those were two things she needed to deal with, so... "How about Wednesday?"

Will gave a slow nod. "All right, then. Wednesday, it is."

"What about the farm? Will you have lambs...?"

"There are always lambs this time of year. If something happens, I'll let you know."

"All right."

"I'll see you then," Will said, and Esther watched as he turned and walked out of the garden, his slow, easy stride so familiar. Then he was gone.

Around her people were standing up and starting to move around, their lunch break finished. The warmth of the day was starting to seep away, a slight chill in the early April air. There was still plenty of work to do, but Esther suspected people would call it a day if she let them. And why not? They'd all worked hard.

"Are we going to have another meeting?" Sophie asked as she helped tidy up the dirty mugs and platters that only held flapjack crumbs. "To organize the planting? And we should probably have a committee of some sort..."

"Yes, we'll definitely need another meeting. I'll sort out the village hall..."

"Why not have it in the vicarage?" Ruth suggested as she picked up a carafe. "It's big enough, and it's far warmer than the hall."

"That's an idea," Sophie chimed in, brightening. "The village hall always smells like stale beer."

That was true enough. "If you're sure, Mum…"

"Of course I'm sure." Ruth smiled at Sophie. "We certainly have the space."

"All right, why don't we make it for next Monday? That will give me time to get a bit more organized. I'll send an email out to everyone."

Sophie nodded, and after they'd tidied up, Esther thanked everyone and people began to trickle away, until the garden was empty, an expanse of freshly tilled earth, admittedly strewn with rocks and twisted roots, but still. It was a start.

A flash of purple amidst the deep, black soil drew her curiosity and Esther stooped to see a few tiny crocuses struggling through the earth. Somehow they'd survived the blades of the tiller, and were now tilting their tiny heads towards the sun. It made her smile, even as something in her tightened. If a little flower could survive having its entire environment chucked about and overturned, then perhaps she could survive this stage of life and loss. Perhaps she could survive having her whole self churned up and overturned, and maybe even be stronger as a result. She could grow and bloom.

Esther crouched down to pat the earth around the crocus and clear away the bits of twisted roots. The least she could do was give the little flower a fighting chance.

Back in the vicarage, her father had closeted himself in the study and Ruth had gone out to visit someone. Esther was just contemplating taking Charlie for a walk when her gaze rested on a card stuck to the fridge with a magnet. *Hope Heals Counselling.* Had her mother put it there on purpose, a not-so-subtle hint? Esther certainly hadn't noticed it before.

She plucked the card from the fridge and studied it for a moment, wondering if she was mad even to be thinking about it. She hated talking about her feelings, and she'd talked about them more in the last few days than she had in years. And here she was, thinking about doing it some more, to someone who she had to *pay* to listen.

And yet... Will's comments unsettled her, mostly because he was right. She had been going through life with a scorecard in hand, always needing to work hard, be the best, and keep control. All things she'd had to give up in the last few months, and that was hard. Her mother had seemed to think counseling could help, and Esther had finally got to the point where trying felt better than simply sitting and staring at the wall, trying to empty her mind out because the jumbled thoughts were too much to take. She'd always felt a need to work hard; perhaps she could work hard at this. Getting better. Moving on. Making her life—and her marriage—work.

Esther slid her mobile phone from her pocket and dialled the number.

She'd just finished making an appointment for the following Thursday, feeling anxious already at the prospect of spilling her guts to a stranger, when Rachel blew in the front door, full of bubbly enthusiasm.

"Esther, are you free? You won't believe it, but we've found the perfect house."

"Have you? Where's Dan?"

"Oh, he had to go to the clinic for an afternoon surgery." Rachel waved her fiancé away with one blithe movement. "Do you want to see it? I can keep the keys for another hour."

"All right." Esther was heartened to see her sister looking so happy. For the last few weeks Rachel had seemed either dour or tense, and so unlike her bubbly self. Perhaps it was simply wedding nerves, but it had worried Esther, and she suspected her mother as well, although as far as Esther knew Ruth had restrained herself from interfering.

A few minutes later, they were in Rachel's little tin can of a car, hardly suitable for the narrow tracks that often got snowed in during the winter, but Rachel had never minded. She stayed in the village or holed up at home if she couldn't get out, and, as she said, if she couldn't get to school, nobody else could.

Now they drove through Thornthwaite, past the pubs and school, all the way to the top by the new estate, and then Rachel turned down a narrow single-track lane that headed towards Windermere.

"How far is it?" Esther asked as fells and forest streamed by. Bunches of blue and purple crocuses were clustered along the road, and a few slightly chilled-looking daffodils bobbed their yellow heads in the breeze.

"A couple of miles. If you go the back way, it's only fifteen minutes to Keswick."

"The back way?" Esther suppressed a smile. "Every way is back way around here."

"You know what I mean. It's perfect, it really is." Rachel let out a happy sigh. "We've been looking and looking and nothing seemed right, you know? But I really think this could be it."

"You sound happier about the house than the wedding," Esther remarked, meaning it as a joke, but Rachel's jerking a little bit made it feel like an insult. Or an accusation.

"It's an important decision," Rachel said after a moment, her gaze fixed on the road, and Esther wondered what she was talking about—the house or the marriage. She decided not to ask.

They drove for a few more minutes, the road curving around dramatically as it hugged the bottom of the fells, and then up a steep little lane so narrow the hedgerows brushed the wing mirrors before they parked in front of a substantial house of classic grey Lakeland stone, with a front porch trimmed in white and a path of flat flagstones leading up to it.

"Wow." Esther unbuckled her seat belt and got out slowly, her gaze on the house. "That's a huge pile."

"It's not so big," Rachel defended. "Only five bedrooms."

"Only?" Esther shot her sister a curious look. "Are you planning on having loads of kids, then?"

Rachel looked startled. "It's a bit early to start thinking about that."

"Is it? Sometimes I think Will and I should have thought about it earlier." Maybe if they'd discussed it more, she would have realized how she felt, and they could have avoided... well, some of the heartache, maybe. Or maybe she could have got over her fear and anxiety, recognized it for what it was.

"Why? What would have changed then?" Rachel asked, and Esther hesitated as she realized she didn't want to get into her whole not-wanting-a-baby thing with her sister. Telling both Will and her mother had been hard enough.

"It's just, things would have been clearer," she said with a shrug. "You both want to be thinking the same things when it comes to the big issues, you know?"

"I know," Rachel answered, but she sounded as if she wasn't really listening as she fished for the keys in her bag. "Let me show you the inside."

The inside was amazing. Esther stepped into the stone-flagged entrance hall, the walls a tasteful pewter that was surely thanks to Farrow & Ball, and then followed Rachel into the sitting room, which had an enormous fireplace and views of Lonscale Fell, and the dining room, with its high ceiling and wood stove.

"But this is the best bit," Rachel said as they walked to the back of the house; the kitchen cum family room spanned the entire width, with French windows that led onto a terrace with a breath-taking view of the fells, Derwentwater glinting in the distance.

"Wow." It was an incredible kitchen, complete with a state-of-the-art Aga, marble counters, and bespoke cabinets. "Is the floor heated?"

"Yes, under floor heating in every room," Rachel answered happily. "We won't be getting frostbite while getting into the bath, the way we did as kids."

"Yet, but…" Esther shook her head slowly. "Rachel, how much does this place cost?" It had to be a very pretty penny. Property in the lake district, even the tucked-away parts, was dear.

"Oh, that doesn't matter," Rachel answered with a shrug as she gazed out the French windows at the incredible view. "Anyway, we're selling both our houses and only buying the one, so…"

"Well, it is beautiful." Esther gazed at her sister, the slightly stubborn jut of her chin, the slump of her shoulders. Something didn't feel quite right, but she didn't know what it was, and Rachel didn't seem inclined to tell her, anyway. But, determined to be different now, she persisted. "Rach… is everything all right? Between you and Dan?"

Rachel stiffened and then turned around, her arms folded. "Of course everything is," she said, a defensive, defiant note in her voice. "Why wouldn't it be?"

"It's just—"

"I brought you here to show you the house," Rachel cut her off, sounding uncharacteristically angry. "Not lecture me."

"I wasn't—"

"I need to get the keys back," Rachel said, and walked out of the kitchen, leaving Esther no choice but to follow.

Chapter Fifteen

"READY FOR DRESS number one, ladies?"

Esther winced both at the sales assistant's obsequious trill as well as the overly sweet cocktail she'd just taken a sip of. It was Saturday afternoon, and she, Anna, and Ruth were all sitting on white faux-leather divans while Rachel tried on wedding dresses. Miriam had joined them by Skype, the laptop set out on a glass coffee table so she could see as much as possible. Her sister had looked tanned and happy and relaxed, a white sand beach visible behind her, quite at odds with the rain lashing the windowpanes of the boutique.

"Yes," Ruth called brightly, her cocktail untouched. "We're ready!"

It had been a week since the garden clear out, and Esther had been busy wrapping up her work with Natural England as well as getting the community garden running, with a lot of help from Sophie West, who seemed keen and energetic and was far more organized than Esther was. They'd opened a bank account and created an official email address, engaged a freelance landscaper, and put a notice in the parish magazine. Sophie had even knocked up a website and had plans for a fundraiser in the summer, "Prosecco and Strawberries" in the vicarage garden. Simon, who would have taken possession of the vicarage by then, had already said yes.

It had also been a week since Rachel had shown her the dream house, and as far as Esther could see, not much had changed there. Her sister still seemed both tense and determinedly happy, which as far as Esther could tell was not a good combination. Esther hadn't seen much of Dan, but when he'd stopped by the vicarage once he had seemed unusually preoccupied, making her worry all the more. She feared there was a little bit of trouble in paradise... but then there was no such thing as paradise, was there? Like both her parents had said, happiness took hard work.

Besides working on the garden, Esther had been getting ready for her big date on Wednesday, which had involved having her hair highlighted, something she'd never done before, and waxing in places she never had before, just in case. Wednesday afternoon had had her looking glossy and new, and it had all been for naught because Will had had to cancel thanks to trouble with one of his new lambs.

Esther had been a bit surprised by how disappointed she had felt. She'd thought she hadn't been all that excited about their date—more nervous, really, but apparently she'd been deceiving herself, because when he'd cancelled she'd been gutted, as well as grateful she hadn't actually told anyone about the date since it wasn't happening.

Will had rescheduled for Sunday evening, but she knew what a farmer's life was like, and therefore, a farmer's wife. She wasn't holding her breath, or onto her hopes.

The following day she'd gone to her first counselling session in Keswick, dreading it so much her stomach had churned until she'd had cramps. But in the end talking about herself hadn't been as hard as she'd thought, even if she'd inwardly squirmed for the entire half hour, answering Claire, the counsellor's well-meaning questions with hesitations and mumbled half-sentences, which hadn't seemed to bother the kindly woman a whit.

It had, Esther had realized after it was over, felt better than she'd expected, sort of like picking at a scab only to realize that what was underneath wasn't as raw and bloody and wounded-looking as she'd feared.

"Has she come out yet?" Miriam asked from the laptop, craning her head as if she could see more from her place on the beach ten thousand miles away.

"Almost," Anna answered with a laugh. "Come on, Rach!"

Rachel, after a flurry of excitement over satin and lace and girly cocktails, had gone ominously silent behind the thick ivory curtain.

"Do you need any help with the buttons?" the sales assistant, Tara, piped up as she twitched the curtains.

Esther glanced at her mother, who was smiling although

there was a faint furrow between her brows, a sure sign she was a bit worried. Despite the air of genuine excitement Esther knew her sisters felt, something seemed a little too forced about the occasion, or at least about Rachel. Or was she just projecting her own dilemmas onto her poor sister?

"Here she is," Tara called, and she swept aside the curtain with a dramatic rattle of rings. Rachel stepped out, smiling tremulously, in an absolute meringue of a dress, the huge white bell skirt engulfing her curvy frame.

"Wow," Anna said after a second when everyone was silent. "It's so…"

"Big," Esther supplied, because how could she not?

"It's awful, isn't it?" Rachel said with an attempt at a laugh. "I feel like Cinderella on steroids." Tara looked slightly affronted by this, but Anna let out a little bubble of relieved laughter.

"Well, I wouldn't say that exactly…"

"Let me see," Miriam demanded from the laptop, and when Rachel stepped in front of the screen, she let out a great, big bellow of laughter. "Definitely, Rach, you look like you're jacked up on egg whites there. Try another one."

"Has Miriam taken over for Esther now?" Anna quipped, and Esther pretended to look offended.

"No, of course she hasn't. Rachel, that dress is hideous and you know it. Or if you don't, you're blind. Try something else."

Their good-natured plain speaking seemed to break the

mood, or perhaps make it, because suddenly everyone was laughing, and more cocktails were poured, and Rachel was smiling as she went back into the dressing room.

"I don't know if Tara appreciated our candour," Anna stage-whispered, and Miriam's voice erupted from the laptop.

"Wait, what? Who's Tara?"

A flurry of laughter, questions, and exclamations later, Rachel emerged from the dressing room in a slinky, diamante-encrusted number.

"Well?" She twirled around, the mermaid-like train of the dress sparkling as it swirled.

"It looks," Ruth offered hesitantly, "like something you might wear after the wedding...?"

Esther snorted and Miriam demanded that Rachel stand in front of the laptop again.

"You do look poured into it a bit," she offered. "You want to be drinking the cocktails, not looking like one. Speaking of... what are you all drinking? I can see it's bright pink but not much else and all I've got here is a bottle of water."

"Poor you," Esther said dryly, and Miriam grinned.

"They're drinking sex on the beach," Tara informed them helpfully, and Ruth looked startled.

"It's not really called that, is it?" she asked.

"No, of course it's not," Anna said quickly, and Esther suppressed another snort of laughter. Ruth gave her daughter a knowing look.

"Don't lie to me," she scolded with a smile. "I'm naïve, not stupid. But why on earth would they call a drink such a terrible name?"

"Perhaps we'd better leave that one unanswered," Esther murmured. Not that she'd know. Cocktails, not to mention literal sex on the beach, were both beyond her range of rather humdrum experiences.

"How about this one?" Rachel stepped from behind the curtain with an uncertain flourish, a tentative smile on her face.

"Oh, Rachel." Ruth clasped her hands together. "You look radiant."

"Doesn't she?" Tara agreed in the trill-like voice she couldn't seem to turn off. "I think this might be the one, ladies."

It was a lovely dress, simple, with a sweetheart neckline, cap sleeves, and intricate lace detailing on the bodice.

"What do you think, Rachel?" Anna asked. "Do you like it?"

Rachel gave a little twirl before staring hard at her reflection. Everyone waited, holding their breath, for her verdict.

"Yes," she said, and she sounded firm, even resolute. "This is the one."

Anna and Ruth both rose with exclamations of delight; Ruth hugged Rachel while Anna snapped photos on her phone, and Miriam kept demanding that Rachel stand in front of the screen. Rachel did, and Miriam pronounced it definitely the one, and then added, with a salacious wink, that Dan wouldn't be able to wait to take it off her.

"Miriam, really," Ruth scolded, but she was smiling.

"What?" Miriam asked innocently. "They're going to be married. Song of Solomon and all that. No one needs to be a prude."

Esther stayed where she was, noting the tilt of Rachel's chin; it reminded her of when she'd been in that enormous house of Lakeland stone, staring out at the fells. She'd looked determined but also a little sad, as if she were holding onto something, afraid to let it go, and Esther felt that same alarming mix of emotions emanating from her sister now, at a time when surely she should feel nothing but joy?

Although who was she to tell anyone what to feel at any given moment? She certainly hadn't experienced emotions by the book.

"I'll just take this off," Rachel murmured, slipping away from Ruth and Anna, her face averted, a tendril of dark hair coming down to fall across her cheek, making her look even more forlorn.

"Let me help you with the buttons," Esther said, rising. She glanced at the fluttering Tara. "Why don't you fetch us some more cocktails? Preferably ones with G-rated names."

"Oh, really," Ruth murmured. "I'm not quite so easily shocked. I have had five children, you know, and one of you was conceived while we were—"

"Stop right there." Anna held up a hand, laughing. "Before I'm forever scarred."

"No, where?" Miriam asked. "Do tell, Mum. Was it me?"

Tara hurried off and Esther followed Rachel into the dressing room, leaving her mother to give—or not—the details of at least one of their conceptions. Shudder.

Alone in the dressing room Rachel bent her head as Esther set to undoing what looked like about a thousand tiny buttons. Neither of them spoke for a few moments, but Esther could feel the tension thrumming through her sister's body.

"Rachel," she said quietly, and Rachel shook her head, the movement almost violent, surprising Esther.

"Don't."

"What do you think I'm going to say?"

"I don't know."

"Somehow I think you do."

"Don't play games with me, Esther. Not now."

"I'm not playing games," Esther answered, a little bit stung even though Rachel had to be raw and hurting, just as she was, or at least had been. She was getting better now, or so she hoped. "I'll say it as plainly as I can, because it seems no one else will. I don't know what it is, but something feels off between you and Dan. Wrong."

Rachel was silent and Esther kept undoing the buttons, fiddly things that they were. "Everyone feels a bit jittery before a wedding," she said at last.

Esther didn't think Rachel was feeling mere jitters. "Your wedding isn't for three months," she pointed out.

"Still."

"Is it really just jitters, Rachel?" Esther stopped with the buttons and straightened, meeting her sister's reluctant gaze in the mirror. "Or is it something more?" Rachel didn't reply and Esther pressed on, determined now. "Ever since the two of you got engaged you've seemed a bit... manic. I mean, you're always a bit manic, but lately it's taken on a desperate edge."

"Wow, thanks."

"I'm trying to help."

"Well, don't." Rachel's voice sounded choked, and Esther's heart twisted; she was filled with equal parts sympathy and exasperation.

"All I'm saying is..." She hesitated, because she knew what she was saying was big. Important, but also hard, the hardest thing of all, both to say and to hear. But someone had to say it, and it seemed like it was going to have to be her. "If you're not sure about this, about marriage or about Dan, then it's best to walk away now and not later, not when the planning gets even more extensive, and certainly not when you've stood in church and said vows—"

"I'm not going to walk away," Rachel said, sounding appalled. "I'm getting married in three months! We've put an offer in on that house, and the estate agent says it's sure to be accepted."

"Forget the house—"

"I'm not going to forget the house," Rachel snapped. "Look, Esther, I appreciate you mean well. But just because your life has fallen apart doesn't mean mine is."

Esther blinked, absorbing the words like a slap. "Wow," she said quietly, echoing her sister's earlier sentiment. "Thanks."

"I'm sorry," Rachel said, and now her voice was filled with tears, and she grabbed Esther's hands. "I'm sorry. That was completely out of line and totally bitchy."

"Well, yes," Esther answered, trying for a smile. "It was. But I haven't been Little Miss Sunshine, have I?"

"You never are." Rachel smiled to take any sting from the words. Esther knew she was teasing. Sort of.

"I'm a bit stressed about things," Rachel said, squeezing Esther's hands. "It's only a week until term ends and it's manic at school, with the Easter fair and a wretched spring concert. And, yes, the house is a bit out of our budget but I'm sure we'll be able to afford it with a bit of penny pinching and it's both of our dream house. Please don't worry about me." Rachel squeezed Esther's hands one last time and smiled, although it didn't reach her eyes. Esther didn't know whether to believe a word she'd said. "I'm fine," Rachel assured her. "Honestly."

Esther nodded slowly, knowing she couldn't push it anymore, at least not without seeming completely heartless and insensitive. "So, is this the dress?" she asked and Rachel glanced once more in the mirror, the unbuttoned dress now falling from her shoulders.

"I think it is."

By the time Rachel came out of the dressing room she was her usual cheerful self, and they spent a hilarious half-hour trying on bridesmaid dresses, each one more naff and revolting than the last, before they settled on the simple gown in navy blue Rachel had had her eye on from the beginning and that everyone liked, even if Miriam claimed it was the tiniest bit boring.

When all the dresses had been ordered and paid for, they headed to a nearby swanky bistro for lunch, the kind of place with overpriced salads and even girlier cocktails than the wedding boutique had on offer. Esther was glad to see both of her sisters looking happy and relaxed, and her mother as well. The mood was light and full of fun, so much so that impulsively, in a move totally unlike her usual self, Esther decided to shock her family with a bit of news.

"Will and I are dating," she said as she leaned back in her chair. A thunderous silence greeted her announcement, as three mouths dropped open simultaneously.

"Dating?" Ruth finally said, frowning slightly. "How do you mean, darling?"

"He asked me out to dinner. On a date." To her surprise Esther realized she was rather enjoying the looks of shock and confusion on her family's faces. She didn't surprise them very often, mainly because she was so predictable and boring. It felt nice to be different, to be the tiniest bit wild. "We're going out tomorrow night." As long as there wasn't any trouble with the farm, something she chose not to add.

"Going out?" Rachel wrinkled her nose. "But you're already married."

"Married people can date," Ruth said with a laugh. "I think it sounds like an excellent idea. Put a little romance back in your lives."

"It's not just about romance," Esther objected, already wishing she hadn't been so reckless as to mention Will and dating. Her mother, not to mention her sisters, were going to get all sorts of ideas, none of which she was sure about.

"What is it about, then?" Anna asked. She looked both sympathetic and interested, and, as usual, as if she couldn't say a cross thing if she tried. Esther unbent a little.

"Just getting to know each other again," she half-mumbled. "Starting over, sort of." Which made things *so* much clearer.

"That sounds wonderful, Esther, really." Ruth reached over and squeezed her hand. "We could all use a reset button sometimes, couldn't we?"

Esther smiled and nodded, grateful for her mother's understanding, but still semi-wishing she hadn't shared so much.

"What I want to know," Rachel said, "is will you or won't you on the first date?"

"Rachel." Even Anna sounded scandalized, although she laughed. Ruth shook her head, her lips pressed together, amusement sparkling in her eyes.

"Kiss," Rachel clarified innocently, and Esther laughed.

Chapter Sixteen

A S ESTHER PEERED in the mirror to put on the lipstick she very rarely wore, her mind hearkened back to the first date with Will ten years ago now, dinner at that little Italian place in Keswick the night after they'd first met.

She tried to recall how she felt, what they'd talked about, but all she could remember was that the linguine had been too oily but the tiramisu had been fantastic. Why couldn't she remember more?

She stepped back, surveying her reflection critically. Mutton dressed as lamb? She'd bought a new dress from a funky little shop in Keswick—a knit dress in dark green that ended a good few inches above her knee. Paired with knee-high leather boots, it was hardly the sexiest thing she'd ever worn—although, on second thought, perhaps it was. But Esther didn't think it said "come hither" as much as "stay awhile." Or something like that.

As for that first date... She did remember walking along Keswick's Market Square with Will, their footsteps naturally falling into a matching rhythm, neither of them saying much but feeling happy, which was pretty much how it had always been, until it hadn't.

"Esther." Ruth's voice floated up the stairs. "Will's here."

Feeling as if she was about sixteen, Esther started down the narrow stairs from the vicarage's top floor. She'd told Will she could meet him at the restaurant, but he'd insisted on picking her up, doing the thing properly. Whatever the thing was.

"Hey." She paused on the bottom step, taking in the freshly-washed sight of him. Will Langley had always scrubbed up nicely. Very nicely, with his hair brushed back from his forehead, his blue eyes looking positively cerulean thanks to the blue-and-white checked shirt he wore—a new addition to his wardrobe, Esther was almost certain—with a pair of dark brown cords that did not, amazingly, have any holes or thin, nubby patches. Also new? Or a Christmas present from years gone by? Either way, it didn't matter. He looked wonderful, and she was very glad to see him.

Conscious of Ruth watching them and her father in the study, no doubt giving them space but maintaining an eagle eye, Esther grabbed her coat.

"Thanks for picking me up," she said as she slipped her arms into the sleeves. "I don't think I've had a date come to the door in about twenty years."

"I like to do a thing right," Will answered. He smiled at Ruth. "Nice to see you, Ruth."

"And you will come for dinner on Sunday?" Ruth said,

making Esther turn around in surprise.

"Dinner?" she said blankly, and Ruth gave her an amused and slightly exasperated look.

"It's Easter."

Was it? Somehow the holiday, which was a highlight of her father's working year, had nearly slipped by unnoticed.

"Do you mind?" Will asked when they'd left the vicarage and he'd opened the passenger door of his Rover.

"Mind what?"

"Me coming for Easter."

It would be incredibly churlish of her to mind, and the truth was, she didn't. "No, it will be nice," Esther said. "We had a roast dinner a few weeks ago with Anna and Simon and Rachel and Dan and... I missed you." She said the last a bit awkwardly.

"Did you?" A grin tugged the corner of Will's mouth as he started down the church lane. "Good."

Was it really going to be that simple, Esther wondered as Will turned out of the village and headed towards Windermere. She had no idea where he was taking her, and was looking forward to being surprised. Were they just going to fall back into life together after one date? Was that all it was going to take?

It didn't seem right somehow. She was afraid, not just of getting into the same old rut she'd been in before, but of Will changing his mind. Of him remembering he was angry with her, and deciding she wasn't worth it. Why was she so afraid? Where had all this fear come from?

She'd asked Claire that, at her counselling session. Why did she, someone from a stable home, with loving parents and siblings, feel so insecure and afraid and *damaged?*

"We're all damaged," Claire had said. "That's what life does to you, no matter how much support and love you have. Some of us just hide it better."

And maybe that was true. Maybe Esther felt damaged because she'd been pretending not to be for so long. Maybe that was what had hurt her. In any case, she was trying to find her way forward now... both in her own right and with Will.

She glanced at him, sitting relaxed in the driver's seat, his gaze trained on the winding road.

"Where are we going, anyway?" she asked.

"You'll see."

"You're not going to tell me?"

"I'm a man of few surprises, so I take them when I can."

She laughed at that, and Will shot her a quick, smiling look. Maybe it was going to be that easy, after all. Maybe, despite what her father had said, some things could be easy.

>>><<<

WILL WAS SO wound up he felt as if he might come apart in a burst of coils and springs, like a broken watch. He felt as if everything rode on this date, whether it did or not. Somehow he had to show Esther he was romantic and loving and that she missed him like crazy. It felt like a lot.

Still, it was going well so far. Esther looked gorgeous, her dark hair in a cloud about her face, her eyes alight. He liked seeing her smile. It made him realize she hadn't in a long time, not properly. Was that his fault? Theirs? He still felt as if he were feeling his way through the dark, stumbling step by step, trying to get to the finish line. The happily-ever-after he thought they'd had but Esther still seemed to be looking for, and damn it, they were both going to find it, even if it killed him. Hopefully it wouldn't.

After another ten minutes of driving, Will pulled into the gravel car park of an old coaching inn nestled right against the fells, a dark-green blur in the oncoming twilight. Its windows were lit up from within, and as they stepped inside its welcoming warmth, the smell of fresh flowers, roasting meat, and log fires enveloping them.

Esther looked around her with pleasure. "This is lovely, Will. I didn't even know this place existed."

"A hidden gem." Dan had told him about the place, thank goodness. He wouldn't have even known what to look for.

"Where are we, anyway?"

"Some little place between Keswick and Windermere, only known by the locals."

"And here I thought I was a local."

A smiling waitress showed them to their table, tucked in

the back of the restaurant, close enough to the fireplace to feel its comforting warmth. Esther looked around in obvious pleasure, inspecting the local artwork on the stone walls, the gleaming, deep grey-blue of the slate floor with the scattered Turkish rugs. It was a nice place, Will acknowledged with relief. Thank goodness.

Esther perused the menu while Will settled in his seat, his mind racing to think of something to say. Here they were, on the date he'd asked for, a way to reset but also to properly get to know one another, since it seemed after all these years they didn't. Why had his mind gone completely blank?

"This is really nice." Esther looked up from her menu, smiling. "Thank you."

"It's all right." And... cue silence. Silence that had never bothered Will, but then he'd grown up in a family of farmers, and had more or less been on his own since he was nineteen. He didn't mind silence, never had. But he felt it now.

Fortunately, the waitress came back and they ordered their meals, drinks and starters and mains all at once, just as they always did, because they never liked having to wait to get the server's attention. It made him smile a little bit, how they were falling into their old patterns. Maybe that didn't have to be a bad thing. They knew each other, no matter how Esther felt now. Will was sure of it. Almost.

"I'll go get your drinks," the waitress murmured. Then

she took their menus and there was nothing to hide behind.

Esther broke the quiet first, and let out a little laugh. "I feel like I don't know what to say."

"You're not the only one." Will grimaced a little. "How's the garden going, then?"

"It's going. It's not going to be a full-time job, but it's a fun diversion for the moment." She propped her chin in her hand. "I'm not sure what I'm going to do with my career, to be honest."

"I'm sure you'll think of something." Really, his insights were breathtaking.

"Yes, eventually. It's strange, to be at this crossroads at my age. I was so sure about everything before. Maybe too sure."

"Sometimes it can be good to have a change," Will said, searching for words. "And a think."

"Yes."

Why was this so hard? The other night, when she'd been on his lap, when she'd curled into him, it had felt easy. The words—and the feelings—had come naturally. Maybe dating wasn't a good idea. Dating his *wife*. Really, what had he been thinking?

"Are you angry with me, Will?" Esther spoke the words quietly, clearly meaning them, and he stared at her in wary surprise. She was fiddling, he noticed, with her wedding ring. As far as he knew, she'd never taken it off. He certainly hadn't taken his off.

"What? Why are you asking me that now?"

"Because of everything. Because I've been so... so difficult, I suppose. And because... because I didn't want to have children, and I never even told you. And the way I said... I didn't mean it so... so personally. But I know how it sounded."

How had he not been supposed to take it personally? But he wanted to be done with it now. "It's done, Esther."

"Is it?" She bit her lip. "You haven't answered my question."

"What question?"

"Are you still angry with me?" She shook her head. "Sorry, this isn't the kind of romantic scenario we were both probably envisioning, but I feel like I have to get it out there before we can move on." She gave a wry little grimace. "Perhaps it's the effect of going to counselling."

"You're going to counselling?" That surprised him. Esther was as buttoned-up as they came, or at least she used to be. Clearly it was all change.

"Yes, I know, surprising, isn't it?" She let out a little laugh. "Mum suggested it, and while at first I wanted to run away screaming from the idea, I realized eventually that it might have some merit. I've felt like I've lost myself over the last few months. I want to find myself again, but not just go back to the way I used to be, if that makes sense. To become someone new, yet someone more me." She shook her head. "Now I'm really sounding crazy."

"No, you're not."

"So are you angry? Seriously?" She met his gaze squarely, as she used to. His plain-speaking tell-it-like-it-is Esther. How he loved her, and yet... Will realized he needed to speak the truth, as well.

"Yes," he said slowly. "A bit."

Esther nodded, looking sad but accepting. "I'm not surprised."

"But I'm angry with myself too," Will said, feeling for the words slowly and choosing them with care. "Because I should have realized something was going on. And I suppose I should have asked you if you wanted to have kids. It was one thing out of many that we never talked about, I guess."

"I don't know if I never want to have children," Esther said slowly. "Although I recognize it's getting kind of late. It's just... I was so scared, Will. And I was surprised by how scared I was."

"And you didn't feel you could tell me." That was the nub of it, wasn't it? Esther hadn't told him and he hadn't had a bloody clue.

"No, I guess I didn't. I felt guilty for feeling the way I did. And I didn't want you to look at me differently. But when... when I saw that scan... when I felt the relief... then I felt even worse. And the guilt kept eating away at me, and I felt as if it was impossible to talk to you because we never talked like that..." She shook her head. "So I understand why you're angry." She spread her hands, letting out a wobbly laugh. "I suppose the real question to ask is, can you forgive me? Can we go on from here, dating or no dating?"

"Oh, Esther." A bloody great lump was forming in his throat, and Will took a sip of his drink to ease it. He didn't want to start bawling like a baby in the middle of the nicest restaurant he'd ever been in. "I've already forgiven you. It's nowt a question of that. It never was."

"There you are, going Cumbrian on me."

"It happens, you know, when I get het up."

They smiled at each other, and, with relief, Will felt as if things were lightening between them. Strengthening. Somehow he'd found the right words, after all, and they'd been easy to say. Perhaps the right words always were.

It became simpler then, for both of them, as they moved the conversation on, talking about the farm and the village and the community garden, and Will chimed in with a few ideas about soil management and landscaping, and by the time their starters came they were drawing diagrams on scraps of paper, and Will thought maybe, just maybe, it was going to be all right. They'd stumble their way through the dark together.

>>>><<<<

ESTHER WAS FEELING the tiniest bit tipsy and really very happy as she climbed back into Will's Rover two hours later. It had been touch and go first, stops and starts with the conversation and more importantly, the honesty, but they'd got there in the end. As for where "there" was... Esther wasn't sure it mattered so much anymore. They were there together.

"So, are you going to ask me out again?" she asked, realizing woozily and belatedly that she sounded rather flirtatious. She decided she liked it.

"I might." Will's voice was a low rumble in his chest, and for some reason it reminded Esther of when they'd first kissed, after their second date. They'd been walking down a street in Keswick and he'd laced his fingers through hers and tugged her towards him, and for a second he'd just smiled down at her before he'd leaned in for a thorough and uncompromising kiss, the kiss of a man who definitely knew what he was doing.

It felt like eons since she'd been kissed. Jurassic ages, and yet it had only been weeks. But it had been longer than that since she'd felt like this, with her stomach fizzing and her heart starting to race. She really wanted Will to kiss her.

They drove in a silence that felt more and more expectant the closer they got to Thornthwaite. Then Will was pulling into the church lane, parking the Rover in front of the vicarage, its darkened hulk reassuring Esther that her parents were hopefully asleep and not waiting by the door.

"I feel like such a teenager," she said with a hiccuppy laugh.

"If you were a teenager, your father would be out on the

front steps."

"He wouldn't—"

"He was with Miriam, don't you remember? Her sixth form ball. She was furious."

Esther laughed. "Of course. We all came over for photos beforehand." Somehow she'd forgotten how bound up Will was with her family. He'd been part of it for ten years. She turned to him, about to say something of what she was thinking, but then she saw the intent look in his eyes, and the way his gaze dropped to her mouth, and her stomach fizzed all the more.

"Well, he's not standing outside the door now," she said softly.

"No," Will agreed, his voice low. "He isn't."

A full minute, or what felt like it, ticked by as they simply stared at each other. Then Will let out a little growling sound and reached for her, and Esther practically scrambled over the seat to get close to him.

His lips came down on hers as his arms came around her body and they were kissing, gloriously kissing, in a way they hadn't since Esther could even remember—and it felt wonderful. Incredibly wonderful, because somehow she'd practically forgotten what a good kisser Will was, and how hard his chest felt, and how much she loved feeling his strong arms around her. She felt safe there. Safe and loved.

They kissed and kissed until they were both breathless, and then Will wrenched away, running a hand through his hair.

"I think we should probably say good night."

"What?" Esther blinked at him as her heart kept thudding. "Seriously?"

"We're dating, remember?"

"We're *married.*"

Will smiled wryly. "We're going back to the beginning, right? I'm serious about this, Esther. I'm serious about you. Let's get to know each other again, properly. No rushing. No falling right back into where we were."

Right now, Esther very much felt like rushing. Like falling. Her blood felt as if it was boiling in her veins, surging through her. But even amidst the clamber of her own need, she heard the still, small voice of common sense.

Will was right. If they rushed into this, into *them,* they'd as likely as not fall back into the same old patterns.

And, she realized, there was something strangely exciting about delayed gratification. So she leaned over and gave Will a lingering kiss, and smiled against his mouth as he gripped her arms hard, steadying her, keeping her at a distance, or maybe keeping her close.

She eased back and he released her, smiling wryly.

"Good night, Esther."

"Good night, Will."

Smiling, she slipped from his lap and the Rover, and walked into the vicarage with a satisfied, cat-like grin still on her face.

Chapter Seventeen

WILL STOOD ON the vicarage steps in his best Aran jumper—one Esther had given him last Christmas—and a pair of new cords, a bottle of wine clutched in his hand. He felt unaccountably nervous, which was stupid, because he'd climbed these steps a thousand times.

Trouble was, it felt different now, and so much more was at stake. He hadn't seen Esther since their date, but he'd been smiling about it for the better part of a week. And now it was Easter Sunday, and they were all going to church together before having one of Ruth's epic roast dinners back at the vicarage. Make or break time, and he didn't think he was imagining that.

Resolutely he knocked on the door, and it was opened seconds later by Anna, looking flushed and happy.

"Will! Come in, come in. You don't have to knock, you know."

He shrugged, half-mumbling, "It seemed right."

"Dad's already over at church," Anna continued, "and I'm just trying to get the Yorkshire batter done before we have to leave."

She beckoned him back towards the kitchen, which was emanating lovely smells of roast lamb. Ruth, dressed in a bright pink shift dress and cardigan, swathed in an apron that said *Kiss the Vicar*, gave Will a big smile and a cheery wave.

"Will, come in! Oh, you didn't have to bring a bottle, but thank you. You know it all goes down a treat." He put the bottle on the kitchen table, looking around as if Esther might materialize from the steamy depths of the cosy room. "Esther's just finishing getting ready," Ruth said knowingly. "But she'll be here shortly. Oh, is that Rachel and Dan?"

Will wandered out to the hall again, just in time to see Rachel pull sharply away from Dan. She turned to Will with an over-wide smile.

"Will! It's so good to see you." She gave him a quick hug which Will returned. It was good to be back at the vicarage, a place where he'd always felt he belonged, but it also felt strange and awkward, considering his and Esther's uncertain status.

Except perhaps it wasn't so uncertain anymore.

"There she is." Dan, who had been looking tense and unhappy after his exchange with Rachel, forced a smile as he nodded towards Esther. "Come on down."

Esther smiled rather shyly, her gaze seeking out Will's. She looked lovely in a knit dress of deep blue, one he hadn't seen before, not that he remembered, anyway. She'd pulled her hair back into a low ponytail and earrings glittered at her ears.

Will cleared his throat. "You look nice."

"Thank you."

Dan and Rachel had melted away, leaving them alone in the hall, and they smiled uncertainly at each other for a few seconds before Esther quickly stood on her tiptoes and kissed his check.

"Happy Easter, Will."

He didn't have time to reply, because Rachel was marching back in, a wicker basket looped over one arm. "Right, you two, break it up. I'm putting you in charge of the Easter egg hunt this year."

Esther turned to her sister, startled. "What?"

"I've always had to do it because I'm the teacher, but it's time you had a go, Esther. You hide the eggs all around the church, and make sure you put the signs up so they know where to go. And most importantly, make sure the Denton twins don't take more than three eggs each. They always try to sneak some, and then some poor little blighter doesn't get any."

"Rachel, you are so much better at this—"

"And, this year, I want a break," Rachel said firmly. "There's time to hide the eggs before church. Anna and I will hand out the chocolate eggs at the door."

"And what should I do?" Dan asked jovially, and Rachel flicked him a quick, inscrutable glance.

"You can hand them out too, and keep the boys in line."

Will glanced at the pair of them curiously, wondering what was going on. Something had to be, if even he could feel the tension in the air. He hoped they sorted it out, even as he felt a treacherous little flicker of relief that his and Esther's problems might not take centre stage, at least for today.

Rachel thrust the basket of eggs at Esther, who had no choice but to take it. She gave Will a bemused glance. "Shall we?"

"All right, then."

Outside the air was still damp from the rain last night, although sunshine was breaking through the wispy shreds of cloud. Everything sparkled and gleamed, the gravel crunching underfoot as they walked over to the churchyard adjacent to the vicarage.

"Right." Esther glanced down at the basket of plastic eggs. "So we hide these and at the end they can exchange them for chocolate ones." She nodded towards the Memory Garden across from the church. "That's as good a place as any, I suppose."

Silently they headed over towards the little space that had been turned into a memorial for lost loved ones years ago, before Roger Holley had taken up his position. Will hadn't been in there much before, and he glanced at it now, taking in the crocuses and daffodils that were just starting to poke up from the damp soil, the rose bushes with buds still tightly furled. Esther had bent to hide an egg on the base of a little stone memorial, but she froze for a second as she read the inscription. Will came over to join her so he could read it too.

In Memory of Our Littlest One. Underneath was an etching of a tiny baby being held in a pair of hands. Staring at the picture and inscription, Will felt as if he'd been punched in the gut. A pain he'd thought he'd dealt with lanced through him, and looking at Esther's face, he knew she felt it too.

She might have been scared to be pregnant, but she missed their baby, the hope of it, as much as he did. He put one hand on her shoulder, and she pressed a hand to her mouth.

"I don't know why I feel sad."

"Seems a natural response to me."

"Yes, but..." She drew a quick, hitched breath and shook her head.

"Look, Esther, I'm no expert, but I think it's normal to feel two things at once. We're complex creatures, us humans, or so they say. Stop making everything so black and white."

"I wasn't even pregnant..."

"Yes, you were. The test came up positive. You had morning sickness. We hoped." His voice came out fierce. "You were scared and yes, relieved, but you're allowed to feel sad, too. Why won't you let yourself?"

Esther let out a shaky sigh. "Because I feel so guilty, I

suppose."

"I'm not the one who can deal with that. You've got to let it go, Esther. Only you can." Will stopped, because he'd said all he could, but at least he could still do something. Gently he pulled her into a hug, wrapping his arms around her as he rested his chin on her head. Esther returned the hug, her cheek pressed against his chest. Will would have been happy to stay that way forever, or at least an hour or two.

The church bell had started to ring, though, and reluctantly they separated. "We ought to make a move with these eggs," Esther said, and Will took a couple from the basket.

"Come on, then. I'll give the Denton twins a run for their money."

⟫⟫⟪⟪

As Esther walked into the church ten minutes later, the eggs all well hidden and Will by her side, something that had been clenched tightly inside her started to loosen.

She breathed in the familiar, slightly musty smell of the church, candle wax and fresh flowers and dust as she caught her father's eye. He was standing by the door to welcome people, dressed in his cassock and surplice, looking as jovial as ever, and Esther's heart twisted with love. What would she have done these last few weeks without her parents? What would she do without them in a little less than three months, when they left?

As if sensing her thoughts, Will slipped his hand into hers and Esther clung to him. Were they back together officially, finally, for good? She didn't know, but she had a good feeling about it. About them. And that was something she'd been waiting and hoping for, for a long time.

They took their places in the front pew next to Ruth and Anna; Simon was up at the front, with Roger, but Esther saw him shoot Anna a quick, loving smile. Dan and Rachel slipped in after them, and then the first few joyous notes of "Jesus Christ is Risen Today" boomed from the organ, and everyone stood up.

As Esther joined in the hymn she'd sung every year since she could remember, the loosening and lightening inside her increased, until she was smiling as she sang. Will had told her she needed to stop feeling guilty, and wasn't that what Easter was all about? The ultimate reset button for humanity, for her. She would never presume or hope to have the kind of faith her parents had, but in that moment, she felt a gentle nudge, a settling of peace. Maybe second chances were possible after all, not just for her and Will together, but for her as a person, a woman, even a mother. She could move on. She could let go.

"Aaa-aaa-aaa-aaa-lei-lu-a," she sang lustily, and Will grinned at her.

Despite their best attempts to hide the eggs in difficult places, the egg hunt after church was a mad scrum. Rachel had given Esther a knowing and rather evil grin as she stepped aside to let Will and Esther manage the proceedings, which they did rather badly and in bafflement.

The aforementioned Denton twins went tearing off before Esther had finished giving instructions, and Will reached one hand out and grabbed one of the ten-year-old boys by the scruff of his jumper. He looked shocked, and started to protest, and Will silenced him with a look. Esther watched, a smile tugging at her lips as a sudden thought slipped into her mind unbidden. *Will would make a great dad.*

Her heart twisted at the thought and she looked away. How could she think that, after everything? And yet she did. The rest of the children raced off and Esther and Will tried to keep up with them, making sure the older ones didn't take too many eggs, or snatch all the easy ones, and she encouraged the shyer, younger ones along. They fell into their roles naturally, with Will keeping a stern eye on the rowdy boys while Esther helped the smaller children.

When a little girl slipped her hand into hers and began to take her around the garden, chattering all the way, Esther's heart melted a little bit. She'd avoided children for the most part, mainly because she didn't think she was any good with them, but this little girl, all of four years old, seemed to have taken a shine to her. As she let herself be led around the garden, she caught Will's eye and he gave her a smile. Her heart caught in her chest; what if he was getting his hopes up? What if she was? Could she cope with that?

After Rachel, Anna, and Dan had all doled the chocolate eggs out, parishioners began to trickle away to their own Sunday dinners and the Holleys trooped back towards the vicarage where Ruth was already busy getting food on the table.

"Six days off," Roger said with relish as he hung his cassock up on the hook on the back of the study door. "My favourite time of year."

"And your last Easter in Thornthwaite," Anna remarked with a sad little smile. "Won't you miss it, Dad?"

"Of course I'll miss it," Roger answered instantly. "We both will, won't we, darling?" He pulled Ruth into a hug despite her squealing protest that something was in danger of burning on the stove. "But new chapters, eh?" Roger smiled at them all, although there was a bittersweet tilt to his lips. "New chapters for everyone."

"Yes," Esther said, the firm tone of her voice surprising her. "New chapters."

The rest of the day passed in a haze of good food and wine, all of them around the table, tucking into a magnificent roast dinner with all the trimmings before managing hefty slabs of homemade simmel cake, followed by coffee and petit fours.

"I can't eat another bite." Simon groaned as he sat back in his chair, one arm around Anna, who looked similarly well fed. Watching them together, Esther wondered if an engagement announcement was in the offing. They seemed so happy and natural together, but perhaps they were waiting for Rachel and Dan's big day first.

A glance at her sister and her fiancé gave Esther a twinge of unease... although Rachel had been her usual bubbly self for most of the afternoon, when caught in an unsuspecting moment, she looked tense, even unhappy. What could be the problem with her and Dan? Dan was lovely, warm and kind and funny, and good-looking as well, in a gentrified kind of way. He was perfect for Rachel... wasn't he? But then, Esther mused, what did she know about what went on behind closed doors?

"Now that you're all here and watered and fed," Roger announced once the last of the petit fours had been scoffed, "we've got a bit of work to do."

"Work?" Anna sat up. "We'll clear up, Mum. You shouldn't be lifting a finger after all that."

"Nonsense," Ruth protested. "But that's not the work your father means, anyway."

"What, then?" Rachel looked intrigued.

"We've got some sorting to do," Roger said easily. "Your mother and I have realized what we can take to China, and what we can't. And we want to make sure all of you get a share in what's staying, so we thought it best to have a bit of a clear-out while everyone was here."

"What?" Rachel sounded panicked. "Already? But—"

"We are leaving in less than three months," Roger reminded her gently. "The tickets are booked."

Esther's stomach twisted unpleasantly, but she stayed silent because she was starting to realize it didn't help either of her parents to express dismay or concern over their move. This was their choice, both of their choice. If they could accept it, then so could she.

"Right, then," she said, rubbing her hands together. "What's staying and what's got to go?"

The next few hours were painfully bittersweet as Ruth brought out all the fine china she'd amassed over the years—platters and plates, serving and chafing dishes, and three sets of sterling silver that had been passed down from various relatives.

"Mum, this is all your best stuff," Anna protested. "Don't you want to keep some of it?"

"There's no point, really," Ruth replied with a small smile. Esther could see this was hard for her, but she was determinedly cheerful. "We can't ship it."

"But what about when you come back from China?" Rachel burst out. "You're not going to stay there forever, surely?"

"We don't know how long we'll stay there," Roger intervened. "However long God wills. But in any case, if and when we move back to England, we won't be living in a pile like this." He glanced around the high-ceilinged dining room with poignant affection. "You all know as well as I do that most of the old vicarages have been sold off. We were blessed to hang onto this place, and blessed too that Simon will be able to live in it. Whatever home we have after Jinan, it won't be like this."

His words seemed to fall in the stillness of the room like stones thrown into a pool. It gave Esther a jolt to realize just how much was changing—not just her parents' move to China, which, like Rachel, she'd assumed was somewhat temporary, but life afterwards. The days in this big, old vicarage, when it had been a bastion of home life and security, were truly over, or almost.

In the end, they divided the china and silver between them, putting some aside for Miriam, who had joined in on Skype and seemed uncharacteristically solemn, watching the proceedings from her usual position on the beach, without any of her usual good-natured jeers and jokes. This felt momentous somehow, far more important and final than throwing out some old tat from the back of the pantry.

Esther came away with a serving platter, a set of sterling silver for four, and the mismatched china teacups and saucers Ruth had inherited from her grandmother. She put it upstairs in her bedroom, unable to keep from noting the incongruity—suitcases and sterling silver, a life in transition. It could almost be art.

Smiling a little, she went back downstairs to help her mother clean up. She found her father by the doorway, waving off Dan and Rachel; Will had already gone, needing to be back on the farm, but, with a sparkle in his eye, he'd promised to arrange another date soon.

The evening was bathed in the shimmering, Technicolor light of early evening, better than any Instagram filter. The grass was touched with gold, the sky so deep a blue it hurt, and yet in a few moments it would start fading to lavender, and the world would begin to grow dark.

"All right there, Bessie?" Roger asked, using a nickname from her childhood that Esther had half-forgotten.

She leaned against his shoulder in a way she hadn't in years, decades, and smiled as the sun began to sink. "Yes," she said, as his arm came around her. "All right."

Chapter Eighteen

"WHAT IS THAT?"

Esther stared at Will, bemused. It was a sunny Saturday morning, nearly a week after Easter, and he was dressed in faded jeans and a fleece, holding what looked like an old-fashioned Dorothy of *Wizard of Oz*-style picnic basket.

Will confirmed her suspicion with a smile. "I thought we'd go on a picnic."

"A picnic?"

"It's a nice day."

"Don't you have work?"

"I can take a few hours off." Will shrugged. "Why not?"

Why not? Because they didn't do picnics. They never had. After those first few dates they'd settled into a sensible routine, watching boxed sets and talking about farming and work. A picnic somewhere up in the fells was far too romantic for the likes of them.

And yet...

"I didn't even think we owned a picnic basket."

"We don't." Will glanced down at the cute basket with the red gingham lining, like something Little Red Riding Hood would have. "I borrowed it."

"You've thought this through, haven't you?"

"I have."

Happiness zinged through her, like a firework. She couldn't remember feeling so light. It had been a good week, working on the garden, helping her parents sort out the house. The uncertainty she'd been feeling was being replaced, slowly but surely, by something solid and good. As cheesy as it sounded, she wasn't just finding her way back to Will, she was finding her way back to herself.

"All right," she said. "Will I need hiking boots?"

"Of course."

A few minutes later she was ready to go, and after calling to Ruth that Esther would be out for most of the day, Esther climbed into the Rover and Will got into the driver's seat, the picnic basket between them.

Sunshine spilled through the windows as they drove out of Thornthwaite and then turned towards Keswick.

"How's the garden coming along, then?" Will asked, and Esther told him about the meeting they'd held at the vicarage a few nights ago, with a committee formed, and a plan for the landscaping in place.

"There will be four small veg plots, as well as a communal space, and two cold frames, and the greenhouse, of course. Sophie's working on a fundraiser in the summer, a strawberries and Prosecco evening in the vicarage garden, with fancy dress, just for fun."

"Sounds good," Will said. "Can I come as a farmer?"

Esther laughed, because Will had never been one for fancy dress. Neither had she, for that matter, but perhaps this time she'd give it a go. "We could go together," she offered. "The farmer and his wife."

Will shot her a quick, searching look, and Esther met it. Yes, she was really saying that. Really feeling it.

"Sounds like the perfect costume to me."

"Not too much of a costume, though," Esther said, her words still loaded with meaning, obvious and important to both of them.

Will nodded slowly. "No, not too much."

He turned off the A66 towards a little B-road that curved around the sparkling expanse of Derwentwater, its placid surface shimmering in the sunlight, the dramatic, dark-green sweep of the fells a stunning backdrop to the perfect scene.

"I thought we could stop near Otterbield Bay," he said as the Rover bumped along. "It's a nice spot."

Soon enough they were pulling into the little inlet, which was surprisingly empty on this gorgeous day, the stretch of grass to the rocky shore pristine and sparkling with dew.

Will laid out a blanket and they both sat down, gazing at the water. Esther felt perfectly content, a settled feeling inside her it seemed almost nothing could shake. Why had it taken so long, so much striving and grieving and fear, to get here? She decided the answer didn't matter; the point was, she *was* here, and so was Will.

Will started unpacking their picnic, and Esther exclaimed over the array of delicacies, "Stuffed olives... Brie cheese... strawberries... *champagne?*" She goggled as he popped the cork on the demi-bottle.

"It looks as if you've cleared out Booth's," she remarked, referencing the upscale supermarket in Keswick.

"Did my best." He handed her a plastic flute of fizz and held his own aloft. "To us, Esther."

"To us," she agreed, and they clinked plastic before taking sips. It felt strange and yet also strangely right to be so romantic, sipping champagne and feeding each other bits of food on a picnic blanket, the kind of thing they'd never, ever done. Esther felt self-conscious but she also felt happy, and it wasn't that bad of a combination.

Then, when lunch was over, Will nodded towards the water. "Dare you."

"Dare me? To do what?"

"Swim."

Esther let out a disbelieving laugh. Wild swimming in the lakes was a popular pastime, but as far as she was concerned it was a crazy one. The water was ice-cold and deep, the bottom rocky and unforgiving. Most people only swam wearing wetsuits.

"Are you serious?" she said. "It's only April."

"End of April."

"Still. I'll turn blue in about five seconds."

Will leaned back, his arms braced behind him. "Chicken?" he jeered softly, his eyes sparkling with humour.

"I'm not chicken, I'm sensible," Esther retorted, and when she saw Will's nod of satisfaction she realized she'd fallen neatly, and oh so predictably, into his trap. She was sensible. Sensible, box-ticking Esther, always with a to-do list and her stupid scorecard. Was Will daring her to be different for once? To be foolish and reckless and even stupid?

"Fine," she said, with an upward tilt of her chin. "Since you want me to be stupid."

"Not stupid," Will corrected with a laugh. "Daring."

She rose from the blanket, and as she walked towards the water, the sun which had felt so benevolent and warm a few moments ago suddenly didn't seem so much anymore. She unlaced her hiking boots and kicked them off, then slipped off her sensible wool socks as well.

"You're not going to go in your clothes, are you?" Will called. "Because that really would be stupid."

"Are you actually asking me to skinny dip?" Esther practically yelped.

Will shrugged, still stretched out on the blanket. "I don't see anyone around."

Esther glanced around, seeing no one but a few walkers in the distance, no more than specks along the horizon. Still, someone could come around the bend at any moment, and she didn't fancy being caught starkers.

"Is this some weird fantasy of yours?" she called back. "Seeing a naked woman freeze to death in the water?"

"Seeing my naked wife," Will returned. "Yes, always. But not freeze to death. Maybe get a bit chilly."

She laughed, shaking her head. Already her hands were at the bottom of her fleece, tugging it upwards. Why was she doing this exactly? She tossed it off, and then shimmied out of her jeans. She could feel Will's eyes on her, even though he didn't say a word.

This was ridiculous, and crazy, and somehow she was loving it. She felt so alive, every sense and sinew singing. Her shirt came next, so she was in her bra and pants. She turned around to face him, her hands on her hips.

"Then I dare you to come in with me," she said, and Will scrambled up from the blanket with alacrity, his hands already on the zip of his fleece.

"I thought you'd never ask."

⤞⤜

WILL DIDN'T KNOW what had possessed him to dare Esther to go into the water; everyone knew how freezing the lakes were, especially this time of year. And yet the bay was shallow, the bottom not too rocky, and they could be in and out in a matter of seconds. There was no real danger, and yet it felt like a risk. A thrill. Perhaps even a baptism.

He pulled his top off and then shucked off his jeans, conscious that walkers could appear on the scene at any moment, and there he and Esther would be, in their underwear. It was so unlike them, and that was why he'd suggested it. It was silly, even stupid, but it was fun and exciting too, and it was new territory for them both.

"So, who is going in first?" Esther asked when they were both standing on the pebbly shore of the lake, a few inches from the water.

"Together?"

"All right."

Will inched a foot in and then couldn't keep from jerking back and shuddering. "Bugger, that's cold."

Esther laughed and splashed him with her foot, the icy droplets spraying his torso. "Now who's the chicken?"

"Not me, woman." Taking a deep breath, Will waded into the ice-cold water. He grabbed Esther's hand and pulled her along with him, and with a screech she followed, both of them splashing into the freezing water until they were chest-deep.

"This is so crazy," Esther said, shivering, and Will pulled her into his arms, their bodies juddering with cold together.

"Crazy but good," he said, and kissed her. She kissed him, the passion they'd felt for each other unleashed once more, and something more than that. Something deeper.

"We're still going to freeze," Esther murmured against his lips, and with a laugh Will swept her into his arms and carried her out of the water. They fell on the blanket together, and Will wrapped them up in it, their wet limbs tangled, toes touching.

Will looked down into her pale, wet face, her lips blue, her eyes sparkling, and his heart expanded with feeling. "I love you," he said, and realized how rarely he said it. He'd never thought he'd needed to, but more than that, he hadn't always wanted to. Not because he didn't love her, but because he hated being vulnerable. And yet here he was, here they both were, and he wanted to say it.

Esther's eyes filled with tears as she gazed up at him. "I love you too, Will," she whispered. "So much."

He kissed her again and her arms came around him, their cold bodies pressed together and warming quickly. Then, in the distance, Will heard an excitable voice.

"Oh, I say, are there otters here?"

ESTHER COMBED HER wet, tangled hair with her fingers, a warmth inside her that belied the freezing dip they'd just taken. After a pair of hikers had stumbled upon them, they'd jumped into their clothes and hightailed it back to the Rover, laughing the whole while. Esther had felt too happy to be embarrassed, and even now, nearly back in Thornthwaite, she felt a bubble of laughter rising in her throat at the memory of the two pensioners suited up in walking gear, holding knobbly walking sticks and nature guides, looks of astonished horror on their faces when they'd come across her and Will. A pair of otters, indeed.

A snort of laughter escaped her and Will grinned. "They won't forget that in a hurry," he said, and she smiled to realize how he'd been thinking the same thing she had.

They pulled into the drive and Will parked in front of the vicarage. He turned the car off and rested his hands on the steering wheel, his expression turning serious. Esther's heart lurched, and then stilled.

"Do you think… do you think you'd consider moving back home?" he asked quietly. There was a raw note of vulnerability in his voice that made her ache.

Esther was silent for a moment, sifting through everything in her mind. Her pregnancy, her relief, her sadness, her uncertainty, the spare bedroom with her suitcases and serving platters. Those crocuses pushing their way up through the tilled earth, small and yet determined. Life on hold, yet ready to begin.

"Yes," she said. "I will."

Back in the vicarage, Esther walked slowly through the rooms, savouring their familiarity as well as the quiet. Yet already things were changing; her parents had given away some furniture, and a few days ago Simon had walked through the house, tellingly with Anna, and picked the pieces he wanted to have stay. Esther had been strangely glad of that; she liked the thought that the vicarage wouldn't be completely different, with some stranger inhabiting its rooms. Simon was practically family, and perhaps soon he would be, judging by the happiness Esther had witnessed between him and Anna.

"Esther?" Ruth came in the dining room where Esther had been standing, gazing sightlessly at the rose-coloured walls with its eclectic collection of art—most of the paintings were done by hobbyist parishioners. "Is everything all right?" Ruth asked.

"Yes, everything is fine. Good, actually." Esther took a deep breath and then smiled. "I've moving back home. To Will's, I mean."

"That is home," Ruth replied with a beaming smile. "Oh Esther, I'm so pleased." She gave her daughter a hug, and Esther squeezed her mother tight, so grateful for her understanding and patience.

"I'm sorry I've been such a pain these last few months," she whispered against her shoulder.

"You're never a pain. And we can't always choose when we feel up or down."

"Yet you said happiness was a choice."

"And one that's not always easy or even possible to make." Ruth eased back with a sigh. "As well I know. I've had some dark days of my own, Esther. And I know that sometimes the only way to get through them is by trudging one step at a time."

"Counselling has helped, actually," Esther admitted, and Ruth's eyes widened in surprise.

"You went?"

"Yes, I took your hint of the card stuck on the fridge." Ruth laughed and didn't deny it. "I never thought I wanted to talk about my feelings, and truth be told, I still don't, but it was okay. It made me realize some things."

"Such as?"

Esther sighed. "That I'm a control freak and a perfectionist and when things don't go my way I pretty much fold." She smiled wryly. "Stuff you and Dad probably already knew."

"We might have had our suspicions," Ruth answered. "But the important thing isn't how or where you've been, but how you are now, and where you're going. And it sounds like you are definitely moving in the right direction, my darling."

It felt strange to pack up her things that evening, and even stranger to put them in her car the next morning, after church. She said goodbye to her parents, feeling like a teenager off to uni, and they both hugged her and insisted she and Will come over for Sunday lunch the following week.

Esther felt both nervous and excited as she made the short drive to the farm, pulling into the yard as rain spattered the windscreen and mist shrouded the fells. Smoke hung in grey wisps above the chimney, the long, low house of white stone huddled against the bottom of the fells. *Home.*

Esther climbed out, leaving her bags in the car, and

walked across the muddy yard to the kitchen door. She opened it slowly, gazing in surprise at the pristine kitchen; the table was cleared of papers and post, and there were no dirty dishes stacked by the sink. It smelled of lemon polish and wood smoke, and it made her smile.

"Will?"

He came clattering down the stairs, sheets bundled in his arms, looking both harassed and hopeful. "Sorry, I was just changing the sheets."

"You didn't have to do all this."

"I wanted to. Welcome home, Esther." She smiled and came towards him, and as his arms closed around her she breathed in the familiar scent of him, sheep and leather and wood smoke. After a few seconds Will eased away. "Someone wants to meet you."

"Someone? What do you mean?"

"Hold on a sec." He disappeared outside while Esther waited, baffled and bemused. A few moments later Will came back in, and Esther's breath caught in her throat. A black lab puppy was squirming in his arms, a pink bow around her neck.

"Oh, Will."

"She's twelve weeks old and has had all her shots. Ready to be my next sheep dog."

"Do labs make good sheep dogs?"

"Good enough." He crouched down and placed the puppy on the floor; she skittered across the tile towards

Esther, sniffing and licking her hands as she bent down to caress her silky ears.

"Oh, Will, she's perfect. I love her." A new puppy could never replace Toby in either of their hearts, but it was fitting to have a new start. A new chapter, just as Roger had said before.

"She'll be a lot of work, of course. Puppies are."

"I've got time." The community garden was virtually up and running, with people applying for the veg plots and the first work day scheduled for the following weekend. As for a proper job… Esther wasn't in any rush, but she hoped a new career prospect would reveal itself eventually, in its proper time. She was learning to trust the process, whatever it turned out to be. Finding out was part of the journey, the pleasure.

After a lunch of soup and bread, Will went back outside and Esther put her things away and played with their new puppy, trying to think of a name for her. While the puppy slept in her basket by the Aga, Esther wandered around the familiar rooms of her home, touching various pictures and piece of furniture, reacquainting herself with the place.

Will had grown up here, and most of the furniture, old and shabby as it was, was from his childhood. The pictures on the walls in the sitting room—a school picture when he was six, his parents' wedding—were so familiar Esther had stopped noticing them. Now she paused in front of an old, eighties-style print of a family gathering, all of them bunched up together in front of the house. Parents and grandparents, cousins and aunts and uncles, it looked like by the number of people, and Esther picked out Will easily, by the shock of hair and the bright blue eyes. Then her gaze fell on a boy she hadn't noticed before—a boy a few years younger than Will, who looked nearly exactly like him. A cousin?

She frowned, wondering why Will had never mentioned any family besides his parents. Why she'd never asked. Perhaps because her family had been so overwhelmingly present, had filled up all the gaps. Now she wondered. She wanted to know more about Will, to discover the depths to him as he had with her.

"Esther?" he called from the kitchen with the familiar stamp of boots. The puppy starting barking.

"I'm in here."

Will came into the sitting room, frowning when he saw her standing in front of the photo on the wall. "What's wrong?"

"Nothing's wrong. I just wondered who this was." She pointed to the boy. "A cousin? You've never mentioned any other relatives before, and I'm ashamed that I never really asked." She smiled at him, wanting to encourage him to share, but her smile wobbled and then faded when she saw him looking so serious. Serious and trapped.

"Will?" Esther prompted uncertainly. "What is it?"

Will sighed and raked a hand through his hair. He nodded towards the photo. "That's my brother."

"Your *brother?*" It was the last thing she'd expected. How could Will have a brother she'd never known about? How could no one, never mind her own husband, have mentioned it?

"Yes. David." He turned away and went back to the kitchen, as if the conversation was already over. Esther's mind spun.

"Will..." She followed him into the kitchen, the puppy tangling about her feet. Will stood by the sink with his back to her as he filled up the kettle. "Why have you never mentioned a brother? Did he... did he die in the accident with your parents?"

"No."

"Then..." She shook her head slowly, still trying to process it. It felt like such a big thing not to know. For the last few months they'd been dealing with all of her emotional baggage, and she'd had no idea that Will might have some of his own. A *lot* of his own. How could she have been so selfish, so self-absorbed? And how could he have kept something like this from her all along? "Where is he now?"

Will didn't answer for a long moment. He looked so weary, his shoulders slumped, his gaze on the farmyard outside the window. "He's in jail," he said at last.

WILL HEARD ESTHER'S quickly indrawn breath and steeled

himself for what came next. He should have told her about David. Hell, he should have told her a long, long time ago, and since he hadn't managed that, he should have told her more recently, when they'd been doing all this soul-baring. But he hadn't, because he'd been afraid. Afraid of her reaction to what he'd done, what he'd felt, just as she had been with him. The irony, brutal as it was, did not escape him.

"In jail?" Esther repeated softly. "Will, what happened? And please turn around and look at me."

So he turned around, slowly, wearily, dreading the next few moments yet knowing he needed to be honest... just as Esther had been honest with him. "David was—is—three years younger than me," he began. "When Mum and Dad died, I had sole care of him."

"That must have been hard."

Will shrugged. "It was what it was." Which yes, had been bloody hard. "David was always a bit wild, getting into trouble at school, and that. Neither of us was ever going to be a great student, but he drank. Did some drugs." He sighed again, the memory of those awful months after his parents' deaths filling him with a familiar blackness. "It got worse then," he explained. "After they died. I couldn't control him, and I tried. Maybe I shouldn't have, but I tried, and he resented it."

"That sounds so incredibly difficult..."

Best to get the worst part over with quickly. "Things

went badly between us. We were always fighting, and I was always angry. It came to a head one night when I realized David had stolen some money from me... money I couldn't spare, because Mum and Dad didn't have any savings or life insurance, and things were tight. He was angry that I was angry, and it blew up in a right storm." Will took a quick, steadying him. "And I hit him. I punched my own brother right in the face."

"Oh, Will."

"And I was glad. I'd been aching to do it for months. He was so furious with me he walked out of the house, said he wasn't ever coming back. And I told him, 'go on, then.' Those were the words I used. Go on, then." Each one stabbed him. "And he did. I haven't seen him since."

Esther gave a soft, shocked gasp. "Not once—"

"A couple of weeks after he left, he got into a fight in a pub. He swung a punch at a bloke and he went down hard. He ended up dying of a brain hemorrhage, and David got seven years for it. He came out again, but just a few months later he got into trouble again, this time a robbery. He's been in jail since."

"Oh, Will. I'm so sorry."

"So am I." He had trouble getting the words out. "I know it was my fault."

When he could bear to look at her, he saw shock on her face. "Will, why do you say that?"

"I hit him. I drove him away." He tried for a smile and

failed. "Seems like a knack I've got."

Esther paled. "Do you mean me..." He couldn't answer. "Oh, Will." Her eyes filled with tears. "I've been so incredibly selfish, so caught up in my own problems, I never thought you even had any. It wasn't your fault. It was never your fault." She strode over to him, wrapping her arms around his middle. "And neither was what happened with your brother. It sounds like it was an incredibly difficult situation, and you were so young..."

"Excuses."

"Now who is the one holding a scorecard?" Esther asked softly, tilting her head up to look at him. "Who's the one feeling guilty when he needs to let it go?"

Will put his arms around her, needing to feel her there. "It's harder than it sounds, I suppose."

"I wish you'd told me."

"I haven't told anyone."

"But people must know," Esther persisted. "Thornthwaite is small, and you've lived here your whole life. Plenty of people must know about David."

"My father's not the vicar," Will reminded her. "And in any case, people around here might have long memories, and they can gossip all right, but they also know when to keep their mouths shut."

"True enough, I suppose." A shadow entered Esther's eyes. "Here I was, feeling like I couldn't tell you things, and I never considered that you might feel you couldn't tell me things."

"I was ashamed," Will said quietly.

"And so was I." Esther pressed her cheek against his shoulder. "But what is love if it can't accept the good parts of someone, the weak along with the strong? You've been so strong for me, Will, and I've relied on you, on that, so much, even when it didn't seem as if I was. You were always there for me, the rock I took for granted. But now I want to be strong for you. That's what marriage is, isn't it? A true partnership, with us leaning on each other?"

He nodded, his chest tight with emotion, his heart full of love. He'd never needed to hear something more. "I suppose that sounds about right," he managed in a rasp.

"I know it does. It's been hard, so hard, getting to where we are now." Her voice caught and she pressed on. "So much heartache and grief and sadness, and I feel like so much of it was my problem, my fault—"

"Hey. Scorecards, remember? We're not having them. They're gone."

"Right." She gazed up at him, smiling although her eyes were troubled. "I don't know what the future holds, whether we'll be brave enough to try for children again…"

"We can cross that bridge when it comes."

"Or whether I'll ever meet your brother…" He nodded gruffly, unable to manage more, but Esther continued with determination, "But I do know that I want to face it all with you. I want to be strong for you, and you strong for me. But

I also want us to be able to be weak, to admit to being weak, to each other." Her eyes lightened as her smile widened. "Do you think we can do that?"

"I think we already have." Will smiled at her, feeling light and happy in the midst of the ache of old, remembered grief. "It's a long road, Esther, and we're just taking a few steps down it. But we're going in the right direction. At last."

"Yes," Esther agreed quietly, a smile blooming across her face like a flower. "At last."

"And now I know what step I want to take," Will said, taking her hand and starting to tug her towards the stairs.

"What..." Esther looked mystified, and Will grinned. He loved his wife.

"I want to go upstairs and remind you that we are married," he said with a deliberately lascivious look. "And get to know you in the biblical sense."

Esther laughed and started towards the stairs. Will didn't know which one of them was more eager to get to the top. They were still laughing as they fell into the big, old bed. Downstairs the puppy barked and Will pulled Esther into his arms. Home at last. Truly home.

Epilogue

Three months later

THE GARDEN WAS full of spring flowers and drowsy bumblebees and laughter as a hobbyist photographer from the parish insisted on taking another full set of snaps. Her parents had been posing for several shots by the trellis, the same place where Esther and Will had taken their wedding pictures.

Will. Esther glanced over at him sprawled in a chair, smiling at the sight of her parents together, and her heart overflowed with love. The last three months had been wonderful, but they'd also been hard, in a good and healing way, as they'd opened up more and more to each other, learning new things, new weaknesses as well as new strengths. Growing closer in a way Esther had never imagined, not even after ten years together. They'd even attended some counselling sessions together, as well as starting to go to church with her parents. Both experiences had been awkward and good. New chapters. New patterns.

Now Rachel's wedding was in just a few days; over the

last few months her sister had forged ahead with wedding plans, seeming more determined than ever. Esther had tried to talk to her on occasion, but Rachel had rebuffed her attempts, and now it seemed things were going ahead, no matter what.

Miriam was due back on the train from Manchester Airport any moment, just in time for all the wedding festivities. This garden party was one of a series of farewells for her parents organized by the church; they were leaving in just a few weeks, after the wedding.

Esther was finally starting to come around to the idea, especially now that the vicarage was packed up, Simon planning to move in as soon as her parents had gone. She'd seen pictures of their small furnished flat in Jinan, and had expressed enthusiasm for her father's new responsibilities. She still dreaded the thought of them not being here, even as she felt happy for the new opportunities and challenges they were facing.

"Miriam!" Ruth's cry rose from the crowd as she separated herself from them and hurried towards the garden gate. Miriam stood there, a rucksack on her back, looking both tanned and exhausted. Rachel, Anna, and Esther all swarmed her, with Roger coming in behind. Everyone was laughing and crying at once; Esther hadn't seen Miriam in nearly two years.

"Easy now." Miriam laughed, sliding the rucksack off her back as she returned all their hugs.

"I'm just so glad you're home, darling," Ruth said, looking tearful, and Miriam smiled.

"Actually," she said. "I'm home for good."

This was met with another chorus of exclamations of surprise and delight.

"I thought you were a diehard world traveller," Will remarked as he came up next to Esther and slid his arm around her waist.

"Were being the operative word," Miriam replied. Her voice was cheerful but Esther thought she saw a trace of sadness in her little sister's eyes, and she wondered if something had happened to make her sister come home for good. If so, Esther thought, Miriam was in the right place to recover and heal—surrounded by family and friends.

They moved back into the garden, and friendly parishioners surrounded Miriam wanting to ask her questions; Esther overheard a well-meaning woman suggest an evening lecture and slide show of her travels for the Over Sixties Club.

Will came to stand behind Esther, and she rested her head against his chest as she soaked in the sunshine.

"Happy?" he murmured, his voice a rumble in his chest as his arms came around her.

Happy? Happiness had been something she'd chased for so long, and had felt so fleeting. The emotion she felt now was far deeper than happiness; it was a mixture of joy and contentment and peace, and it permeated her right down to her bones. To her soul.

Whatever lay ahead, whether it was ease and pleasure or trouble or sorrow, or most likely, a fair bit of both, she was ready for it. Ready, with Will by her side.

"More than happy," she told him, and Will put his arms around her and squeezed, which was all the answer she needed.

THE END

Read Rachel's story next, in A Vicarage Wedding,
out in June 2018!

The Holley Sisters of Thornthwaite Series

Book 1: *A Vicarage Christmas*
Anna's story

Book 2: *A Vicarage Reunion*
Esther's story

Book 3: *A Vicarage Wedding*
Rachel's story

Available now at your favorite online retailer!

About the Author

After spending three years as a diehard New Yorker, **Kate Hewitt** now lives in the Lake District in England with her husband, their five children, and a Golden Retriever. She enjoys such novel things as long country walks and chatting with people in the street, and her children love the freedom of village life—although she often has to ring four or five people to figure out where they've gone off to.

She writes women's fiction as well as contemporary romance under the name Kate Hewitt, and whatever the genre she enjoys delivering a compelling and intensely emotional story.

You can find out more about Katharine on her website at kate-hewitt.com.

Thank you for reading

A Vicarage Reunion

If you enjoyed this book, you can find more from all our great authors at TulePublishing.com, or from your favorite online retailer.

TULE
PUBLISHING

29601032R00160

Printed in Great Britain
by Amazon